PRINCESS IN PERIL

Fou-tan struggled to release herself, but she was utterly helpless in the grasp of her gigantic captor. She tried to wrench the creature's hand from her mouth to scream a warning to Gordon King, but even in this she was doomed to failure.

The creature had a hideous face, with thick lips and protruding teeth, great ears that flapped as he ran, and a low, receding forehead hidden by filthy, tangled hair that almost met the bushy eyebrows beneath which gleamed wicked, bloodshot eyes. It did not require a second look to convince Fou-tan that she had fallen into the hands of one of the dreaded Yeacks . . .

THE LAND
OF
HIDDEN
MEN

Edgar Rice Burroughs

A Del Rey Book
BALLANTINE BOOKS • NEW YORK

A Del Rey Book
Published by Ballantine Books

First published under the title
  JUNGLE GIRL
  Copyright © 1931 by Edgar Rice Burroughs, Inc.

All rights reserved under International and Pan-American Copyright Conventions. Authorized Edgar Rice Burroughs, Inc., edition published in the United States of America by Ballantine Books, a division of Random House, Inc., New York, and simultaneously in Canada by Random House of Canada Limited, Toronto.

ISBN 0-345-37837-7

This edition published by arrangement with Edgar Rice Burroughs, Inc.

Manufactured in the United States of America

First Ballantine Books Edition: November 1992

Cover Art by Michael Herring. Copyright © 1992 by Edgar Rice Burroughs, Inc.

1

❦

The Jungle

"My Lord, I may go no farther," said the Cambodian.

The young white man turned in astonishment upon his native guide. Behind them lay the partially cleared trail along which they had come. It was overgrown with tall grass that concealed the tree-stumps that had been left behind the axes of the road-builders. Before them lay a ravine, at the near edge of which the trail ended. Beyond the ravine was the primitive jungle untouched by man.

"Why, we haven't even started yet!" exclaimed the white man. "You cannot turn back now. What do you suppose I hired you for?"

"I promised to take my lord to the jungle," replied the Cambodian. "There it is. I did not promise to enter it."

Gordon King lighted a cigarette. "Let's talk this thing over, my friend," he said. "It is yet early morning. We can get into the jungle as far as I care to go and out again before sundown."

The Cambodian shook his head. "I will wait for you here, my lord," he said; "but I may not enter the jungle, and if you are wise you will not."

"Why?" demanded King.

"There are wild elephants, my lord, and tigers," replied the Cambodian, "and panthers which hunt by day as well as by night."

"Why do you suppose we brought two rifles?" demanded the white. "At Kompong-Thom they told me you were a good shot and a brave man. You knew that we should have no need for rifles up to this point. No, sir, you have lost your nerve at the last minute, and I do not believe that it is because of tigers or wild elephants.''

"There are other things deep in the jungle, my lord, that no man may look upon and live.''

"What, for example?'' demanded King.

"The ghosts of my ancestors,'' answered the Cambodian, "the Khmers who dwelt here in great cities ages ago. Within the dark shadows of the jungle the ruins of their cities still stand, and down the dark aisles of the forest pass the ancient kings and warriors and little sad-faced queens on ghostly elephants. Fleeing always from the horrible fate that overtook them in life, they pass for ever down the corridors of the jungle, and with them are the millions of the ghostly dead that once were their subjects. We might escape My Lord the Tiger and the wild elephants, but no man may look upon the ghosts of the dead Khmers and live.''

"We shall be out before dark,'' insisted King.

"They are abroad both by day and by night,'' said the Cambodian. "It is the curse of Siva, the Destroyer.''

King shrugged his shoulders, stamped out his cigarette and picked up his rifle. "Wait for me here, then,'' he said. "I shall be out before dark.''

"You will never come out,'' said the Cambodian.

Beyond the ravine, savage, mysterious, rose the jungle, its depth screened from view by the spectral trunks of fromagers and a tangle of bamboo. At first the man could find no opening in that solid wall of vegetation. In its sheath, at his side, hung a heavy knife, but already the young day was so oppressively hot that the man did not relish the idea of exhausting himself at the very outset of his adventure if he could find some easier way. That it would be still hotter he knew, for Cambodia lies but twelve degrees above the equator in the same latitude as Nicaragua, the Sudan, and other places infamous for their heat.

Along the edge of the ravine he searched, until at last he was rewarded by what appeared to be not by any means a trail but a far less formidable growth of bamboo through which he saw that he might easily force his way. Glancing back, he saw his Cambodian guide squatted upon his heels in mournful meditation. For an instant the young man hesitated, as though he was of a mind to try again to persuade the Cambodian to accompany him; but, as though immediately conscious of the futility of any such appeal, he turned again and pushed his way into the jungle.

He had advanced but a short distance when the heavy undergrowth gave way to a much more open forest. The spreading branches of the lofty trees cast upon the ground a perpetual shade, which had discouraged a heavy growth of underbrush.

How different looked the jungle from any picture that his imagination had conjured! How mysterious, but above all, how gloomy and how sinister! A fitting haunt, indeed, for the ghosts of weeping queens and murdered kings. Beneath his breath King cursed his Cambodian guide. He felt no fear, but he did feel an unutterable loneliness.

Only for a moment did he permit the gloom of the jungle to oppress him. He glanced at his watch, opened his pocket compass, and set a course as nearly due north as the winding avenues of the jungle permitted. He may have realised that he was something of a fool to have entered upon such an adventure alone; but it was doubtful that he would have admitted it even to himself, for, indeed, what danger was there? He had, he thought, sufficient water for the day; he was well armed and carried a compass and a heavy knife for trail-cutting. Perhaps he was a little short on food, but one cannot carry too heavy a load through the midday heat of a Cambodian jungle.

Gordon King was a young American who had recently graduated in medicine. Having an independent income, he had no need to practice his profession; and well realising, as he did, that there are already too many poor doctors in the world, he had decided to devote himself for a number of years to the study of strange maladies. For the moment he had permitted himself to be lured from his hobby by the intriguing mysteries of the Khmer ruins of Angkor—ruins that had worked so mightily upon his imagination that it had been impossible for him to withstand the temptation of some independent exploration on his own account. What he expected to discover he did not know; perhaps the ruins of a city more mighty than Angkor Thom; perhaps a temple of greater magnificence and grandeur than Angkor Vat; perhaps nothing more than a day's adventure. Youth is like that.

The jungle that had at first appeared so silent seemed to awaken at the footfall of the trespasser; scolding birds fluttered above him, and there were monkeys now that seemed to have come from nowhere. They, too, scolded as they hurtled through the lower terraces of the forest.

He found the going more difficult than he had imagined, for the floor of the jungle was far from level. There were gulleys and ravines to be crossed and fallen trees across the way, and always he must be careful to move as nearly north as was physically possible, else he might come out far from his Cambodian guide when he sought to return. His rifle grew hotter and heavier; his canteen of water insisted with the perversity of inanimate objects in sliding around in front and bumping him on the belly. He reeked with sweat, and yet he knew that he could not have come more than a few miles from the point where he had left his guide. The tall grasses bothered him most, for he could not see what they hid; and when a cobra slid from beneath his feet and glided away, he realised more fully the menace of the grasses, which in places grew so high that they brushed his face.

At the end of two hours King was perfectly well assured that he was a fool to go on, but there was a certain proportion of bulldog stubbornness in his make-up that would not permit him to turn back so soon. He paused and drank from his canteen. The water was warm and had an unpleasant taste. The best that might be said of it was that it was wet. To his right and a little ahead sounded a sudden crash in the jungle. Startled, he cocked his rifle and stood listening. Perhaps a dead tree had fallen, he thought, or the noise might have been caused by a wild elephant. It was not a ghostly noise at all, and yet it had a strange effect upon his nerves, which, to his disgust, he suddenly realised were on edge. Had he permitted the silly folk tale of the Cambodian to so work upon his imagination that he translated into a suggestion of impending danger every unexpected interruption of the vast silence of the jungle?

Wiping the sweat from his face, he continued on his way, keeping as nearly a northerly direction as was possible. The air was filled with strange odours, among which was one more insistent than the others—a pungent, disagreeable odour that he found strangely familiar and yet could not immediately identify: Lazy air currents, moving sluggishly through the jungle, occasionally brought this odour to his nostrils, sometimes bearing but a vague suggestion of it and again with a strength that was almost sickening; and then suddenly the odour stimulated a memory cell that identified it. He saw himself standing on the concrete floor of a large building, the sides of which were lined with heavily barred cages in which lions and tigers paced nervously to and fro or sprawled in melancholy meditation of their lost freedom; and in his nostrils was the same odour that impinged upon them now. However, it is one thing to contemplate tigers from the safe side of iron bars, and it is quite another thing suddenly to realise their near presence unrestrained by bars of any sort. It occurred to him now that he had not previously considered tigers as anything more serious than a noun; they had not represented a concrete reality. But that mental conception had passed now, routed by the odour that clung in his nostrils. He was not afraid; but realising for the first time, that he was in actual danger, he advanced more warily, always on the alert.

Some marshy ground and several deep ravines had necessitated various detours. It was already almost noon, the time upon which he was determined he must turn back in order that he might reach the point where he had left his guide before darkness fell upon the jungle. Constantly for some time there had lurked within his consciousness a question as to his ability to back-track upon his trail. He had had no experience in woodcraft, and he had already found it far more difficult than he had imagined it would be to maintain a true course by compass; nor had he taken the precautions to blaze his trail in any way, as he might have done by marking the trees with the heavy trail cutter that he carried.

Gordon King was disgusted with himself; he had found no ruins; he was hot, tired and hungry. He realised that he had lost all interest in ruins of any and all descriptions, and after a brief rest he turned back towards the south. It was then, almost immediately, that he realised the proportions of the task that lay ahead of him. For six hours he had been plodding deep into the jungle. If he had averaged two miles an hour, he had covered a distance of twelve miles. He did not know how fast he had walked, but he realised that twelve miles was bad enough when he considered that he had started out fresh and well fortified by a hearty breakfast and that he was returning empty, tired, and footsore.

However, he still believed that he could make the distance easily before dark if he could keep to the trail. He was well prepared physically by years of athletic training, having been a field and track man at college. He was glad now that he had gone in for long distance running; he had won a marathon or two and was never appalled at the thought of long distances to be covered on foot. That he could throw the javelin and hurl the discus to almost championship distances seemed less helpful to him in an emergency of the present nature than his running experience. His only regret on this score was that during the year that he had been out of college he had permitted himself to become soft—a condition that had become increasingly noticeable with every mile that he put behind him.

Within the first minute that Gordon King had been upon the back-trail toward his guide he had discovered that it was absolutely impossible for his untrained eyes to find any sign of the trail that he supposed he had made coming in. The way that he thought he had come, his compass told him, let towards the south-west; but he could find no directing spoor.

With a shake of his head, he resorted again to his compass; but due south pointed into a dense section of jungle through which he was positive he had not come. He wondered whether he should attempt to skirt every obstacle, thereby making long and wide detours or continue straight toward the south, deviating from his direct line only when confronted by insurmountable obstacles. The latter, he felt, would be the shortest way out of the jungle in point of distance, and he was confident that it would bring him as close to his Cambodian guide as any other route that he might elect to follow.

As he approached the patch of jungle that had seemed at first to bar his way completely, he found that it was much more open than he had suspected and that, while the trees were large and grew rather close together, there was little or no underbrush. Glancing often at his compass, he entered the gloomy forest. The heat, which had grown intense, possibly aggravated the fatigue which he now realised was rapidly attaining the proportions of a real menace. He had not appreciated when he stepped out upon this foolish adventure how soft his muscles had become, and as he contemplated the miles and hours of torture that lay ahead of him, he suddenly felt very helpless and alone.

The weight of his rifle, revolver, ammunition, and water represented a definite handicap that he knew might easily defeat his hope of escaping from the jungle before dark. The smell of the great cats was heavy in the air. Against this ever-present premonition of danger, however, was the fact that he had already spent over six hours in the jungle without having caught a glimpse of any of the dread Carnivora. He was convinced, therefore, that he was in little danger of attack by day and that he might have a better chance of getting out of the jungle before dark if he discarded his weapons, which would unquestionably be useless to him after dark.

And then again, he argued, perhaps, after all, there were no man-eaters in the jungle, for he had heard that not all tigers were man-eaters. For the lesser cats, the panthers and leopards, he did not entertain so great a fear, notwithstanding the fact that he had been assured that they were quite as dangerous as their larger cousins. The size, the reputation and the fearful mien of My Lord the Tiger dwarfed his estimate of the formidable nature of the others.

A large, flat stone, backed by denser foliage, suggested that he rest for a moment while deliberating upon the wisdom of abandoning his weapons. The canteen of water, with its depleted store of warm and unpleasant-tasting liquid, he knew he must cling to until it had been emptied. Before he sat down upon the stone he leaned his rifle against a tree, and unbuckling the belt which supported his revolver and also held his ammunition, he tossed it upon the ground at his feet. What a relief! Instantly there left him the fear that he might not be able to get out of the jungle before dark. Relieved of what had become a constantly increasing burden, he felt like a new man and equal to any efforts that the return march might demand of him. He seated himself upon the flat rock and took a very small swallow from the contents of his canteen. He had been sparing of his water and he was glad that he had been, for now he was convinced that it would last him through the remainder of the day, giving him strength and refreshment when he would most need them.

As he replaced the screw cap upon his canteen, he chanced to glance at the rock upon which he was sitting and for the first time was struck by the fact that it seemed incongruously out of place in the midst of this jungle of great trees and foliage. Idly he brushed an accumulation of leaf mould from its surface, and what he saw revealed beneath increased his curiosity sufficiently to cause him to expose the entire surface of the rock, disclosing in bold bas-relief the head and shoulders of a warrior.

Here, then, was the reward for which he had struggled; but he found that it left him a little cold. His interest in Khmer ruins seemed to have evaporated beneath the torrid heat of the jungle. However, he still maintained sufficient curiosity to speculate upon the presence of this single relic of the past. His examination of the ruins of Angkor Thom suggested that this must have been a part of some ancient edifice and if this were true the rest must be close at hand—

perhaps just behind the screen of jungle that formed the background of this solitary fragment.

Rising, he turned and tried to peer through the foliage, separating the leaves and branches with his hand. A few hours before his heart would have leaped at what he glimpsed vaguely now through the leafy screen—a vast pile of masonry through whose crumbling arches he saw stately columns still defying the ruthless inroads of the jungle in the lonely, hopeless battle they had been waging through the silent centuries.

And then it was that, as he stood gazing, half-fascinated by the tragic magnificence that still clung to this crumbling monument to the transient glories and the vanities of man, his eye was attracted by a movement within the ruins; just a glimpse he got where a little sunlight filtered through a fallen roof—a little patch of fawn with dark brown stripes. In the instant that he saw it, it was gone. There had been no sound, just a passing of something among the ruins. But Gordon King felt the cold sweat upon his brow as hastily he gathered up his belt and buckled it about his waist and seized his rifle. Blessed weight! He thanked God that he had not gone on without it.

Forgotten were the ruins of the Khmers as he strode cautiously on through the forest, constantly alert now, looking to the right and to the left, and turning often a hasty glance behind him. Soft are the pads of the carnivores. They give forth no sound. When the end came, if it did come, he knew that there would be a sudden rush and then the terrible fangs and talons. He experienced the uncanny sensation of unseen eyes upon him. He was sure that the beast was stalking him. It was maddening not to be able to see it again.

He found it necessary to consult his compass frequently in order to keep to his course. His instrument was a small one, constructed like a hunting-case watch. When the catch was released the cover flew open, releasing the needle, which, when the cover was closed, was locked in position, that its bearings might not be injured by sudden changes of position.

King was on the point of checking his direction; but as he

held the compass open in his hand, he thought that he heard
a slight noise behind him. As he glanced back the toe of his
boot struck a rock; and trying to regain his equilibrium, he
stumbled into a patch of tumbled sandstone rocks, among
which he sprawled heavily upon his face. Spurred by thoughts
of the sound that he had heard behind him, he scrambled
quickly to his feet; but though he searched the jungle as far
as his eyes could reach in every direction, he could discern
no sign of any menacing beast.

When he had fallen he had dropped his compass, and now
that he was satisfied that no danger lurked in his immediate
vicinity, he set about to recover the instrument. He found it
quickly enough, but one glance at it sent his heart into his
boots—his compass was broken beyond possibility of repair.
It was several seconds before the full measure of this calam-
ity unfolded itself to his stunned consciousness.

For a moment Gordon King was appalled by the accident
that had befallen him, for he knew that it was a real catastrophe. Practically unversed in woodcraft, he found himself in
a jungle overhung by foliage so dense that it was impossible
to get his bearings from the sun, menaced by the ever-present
danger of the great cats and faced with what he felt now was
definite assurance that he would have to spend the night in
these surroundings with only a remote likelihood that he ever
would be able to find his way out in the event that he did not
fall prey to the carnivores or to thirst.

But only momentarily did he permit himself to be crushed
by contemplation of his predicament. He was well armed,
and he knew that he was resourceful and intelligent. Suddenly there came to him a realisation of something that gave
him renewed strength and hope.

Few men know until they are actually confronted by lethal
danger whether at heart they are courageous or cowardly.
Never before had Gordon King been called upon to make
such an appraisal of himself. Alone in this mysterious forest,
uninfluenced by the possibilities of the acclaim or reproaches
of another, there was borne in upon his consciousness a definite realisation of self-sufficiency. He fully realised the dan-

gers that confronted him; he did not relish them, but he felt no sensation of fear.

A new feeling of confidence pervaded him as he set out again in the direction that he had been going before he had fallen and broken his compass. He was still alert and watchful, but he did not glance behind him as much as he had previously. He felt that he was making good headway, and he was sure that he was keeping a true course toward the south. Perhaps, after all, he would get out before dark, he thought. The condition that irritated him most was his increasing thirst, against which he was compelled to pit every ounce of his will power that he might conserve the small amount of water that remained in his canteen.

The route he was following was much more open than that along which he had entered the jungle, so that he was buoyantly hopeful that he would come out of his predicament and the jungle before night had enveloped the gloomy haunt of the great cats; yet he realised that at best he would win by but a small margin.

He was very tired now, a fact that was borne in upon him by the frequency with which he stumbled, and when he fell he found that each time it was only with increased effort that he rose again to his feet. He was rather angry with himself for this seeming weakness. He knew that there was only one thing that he could do to overcome it, and that thing he could not afford to do, for the fleeting minutes of precious daylight would not pause in their flight while he rested.

As the miles fell slowly and painfully behind him and the minutes raced as though attempting to escape him and leave him to the mercy of the darkness and the tigers, the hope that had been newborn in him for a while commenced to desert him; yet he stumbled wearily on, wondering if the jungle had no end and hoping against hope that beyond the next wall of verdure he would break through into the clearing that would mean life and food and water for him.

"It can't be far now," he thought, "and there must be an hour of full daylight ahead." He was almost exhausted; a little rest would renew his strength, he knew, and there, just ahead of him, was a large, flat rock. He would rest for a moment upon it and renew his strength.

As he seated himself upon this hard resting-place, something upon its surface caught his horrified gaze. It was the head and shoulders of a warrior, cut in bold bas-relief.

2

The Delirium

There are circumstances in which even the bravest of men experience a hopelessness of utter despair. Such was King's state of mind when he realised that he had wandered in an aimless circle since noon and was back again at his starting-point. Weakened by physical exhaustion and hunger, he contemplated the future with nothing but pessimism. He had had his chance to escape from the jungle, and he had failed. There was no reason to believe that another day might bring greater opportunity. Rest might recoup his strength slightly, but what he needed was food, and on the morrow he would set forth not with a canteen full of water, but with only a few drops with which to moisten his parched throat. He had stumbled through plenty of mud-holes during the day, but he knew that it would doubtless prove fatal to drink from such wells of pollution.

As he stood there with bowed head, searching his mind for some solution of his problem, his eyes gradually returned to focus, and as they did so he saw on the surface of the soft ground beneath his gaze something that, for the moment, drove thoughts of hunger and thirst and fatigue from his mind—it was the pug of a tiger, fresh made in the soft earth.

"Why worry about to-morrow?" murmured King. "If half what that Cambodian told me about this place at night is true, I'll be in luck if I see another to-morrow."

He had read somewhere that tigers started to hunt late in the afternoon, and he knew that they seldom climbed trees; but he was also aware of the fact that leopards and panthers do and that the latter, especially, on account of their size and inherent viciousness, were fully as much to be dreaded as My Lord the Tiger himself. Realising that he must find some sort of shelter as quickly as possible and recalling the ruins that he had seen through the screen of foliage behind the rock before which he stood, he parted the leafy screen ahead of him and forced his way through.

Here the vegetation was less dense, as though the lesser growth of the jungle had halted in fearful reverence before this awe-inspiring work of man. Majestic even in its ruin was the great rectangular pile that loomed clearly now before the eyes of the American. But not all of the jungle had feared to encroach upon its sanctity. Great trees had taken root upon its terraced walls, among its columns and its arches, and by the slow and resistless pressure of their growth had forced aside the supporting foundation and brought much of the edifice into complete ruin.

Just before him rose a tower that seemed better to have withstood the ravages of time than other portions of the building. It rose some sixty feet above the ground, and near the summit was carved in heroic size the face of a god that King suspected was Siva, the Destroyer. A few feet above the rectangular doorway was a crumbling ledge and just above that a smaller opening that might have been a window. Behind it all was dark, but it carried to King's mind the suggestion of a hiding-place—a sanctuary in the very bosom of Siva.

The face of the weather-worn tower offered sufficient foothold for an agile climber, and the way was made easier by the corbelled construction that supported a series of bas-reliefs rising one above another from the ground level to the edge above the doorway. It was not, however, without considerable difficulty that King, already almost exhausted, finally reached the ledge, where he sat down for a moment's rest. Just above him was the opening which he wished to investigate. As he let his thoughts precede him in that investigation of this possible refuge, they discovered, as thoughts are prone to do, enough unpleasant possibilities to cast a pall of gloom over him. Doubtless it was the den of a panther.

What more secluded spot could this horrid beast discover in which to lie up after feeding or in which to bear and rear its young?

The suggestion forced him to immediate action. He did not believe that there was any panther there, but he could not endure the suspense of doubt. Cocking his rifle, he arose and approached the opening, the lower sill of which was just about level with his breast as he stood upon the ledge above the doorway. Within all was black and silent. He listened intently. If there were anything hiding there, he should hear it breathe; but no sound broke the utter silence of the tomb-like vault. Pushing his rifle ahead of him, King climbed to the sill, where he remained in silence for a moment until his eyes became accustomed to the gloom of the interior, which was slightly relieved by light filtering in through a crack at one side. A few feet below him was a stone floor, and he could see dimly now that the chamber extended the full breadth and width of the tower. In the centre of the apartment rose something, the nature of which he could not distinguish; but he was sure that it was inanimate.

Stepping down to the floor and advancing cautiously, his rifle ready, King made a complete circuit of the walls. There was no panther there, nor any signs that one ever had been there. Apparently the place had never been entered by any creature since that day of mystery, centuries gone, when the priests and temple girls had departed never to return. Turning toward the object in the centre of the room, King quickly identified it as the symbol of Siva and realised that he was doubtless in the Holy of Holies.

Walking back to the window, he seated himself upon the sill, took a small swallow from his scant store of water and lighted a cigarette; and as the sudden night fell upon the jungle, he heard the crisp fall of padded feet upon dry leaves in the courtyard of the temple beneath him.

His position, well above the floor of the jungle, imparted a feeling of security; and the quiet enjoyment of a cigarette soothed his nerves and, temporarily at least, allayed the gnawing pangs of hunger. He derived a form of mild enjoyment by speculating upon the surprise and consternation of his friends could they visualise his present situation. Perhaps uttermost in his thoughts was Susan Anne Prentice, and he knew that he would be in for a good scolding could she be aware of the predicament into which his silly and ill-advised adventure had placed him.

He recalled their parting and the motherly advice she had given him. What a peach of a girl Susan Anne was! It seemed strange to him that she had never married, for there were certainly enough eligible fellows always hanging around her. He was rather glad that she had not, for he realised that he should feel lost without the promise of her companionship when he returned home. He had known Susan Anne as far back as he could remember, and they had always been pals. In the city of their birth their fathers' grounds adjoined and there was no fence between; at the little lake where they spent their summers they were next-door neighbours. Susan Anne had been as much a part of Gordon King's life as had his father or his mother, for each was an only child and they had been as close to one another as brother and sister.

He remembered telling her, the night before he had left home for this trip, that she would doubtless be married by the time he returned. "No chance," she had said with an odd little smile.

"I do not see why not," he had argued. "I know at least half a dozen men who are wild about you."

"Not the right one," she had replied.

"So there is someone?"

"Perhaps."

He wondered who the fellow could be and decided that he must be an awful chump not to appreciate the wonderful qualities of Susan Anne. In so far as looks were concerned, she had it on all the girls of his acquaintance, in addition whereto she had a good head on her shoulders and was a regular fellow in every other respect. Together they had often bemoaned the fact that she was not a man, that they might have palled around on his wanderings together.

His reveries were blasted by a series of low, coughing

roars down there somewhere in the darkness at a little distance from the ruins. They were followed by a crashing sound, as of a large body dashing through underbrush. Then there was a scream and a thud, followed by low growls and silence. King felt his scalp tingle. What tragedy of the jungle night had been enacted in that black, mysterious void?

The sudden and rather terrifying noise and its equally abrupt cessation but tended to impress upon the man and to accentuate the normal, mysterious silence of the jungle. He knew that the jungle teemed with life; yet, for the most part, it moved as silently as might the ghosts of the priests and the temple girls with which imagination might easily people this crumbling ruin of the temple of the Destroyer. Often from below him and from the surrounding jungle came the suggestion of noises—furtive, stealthy sounds that might have been the ghosts of long-dead noises. Sometimes he could interpret these sounds as the cracking of a twig or the rustling of leaves beneath a padded paw, but more often there was just the sense of things below him—grim and terrible creatures that lived by death alone.

And thus the night wore on, until at last day came. He had dozed intermittently, sitting upon the window ledge with his back against its ancient stone frame, his rifle across his lap. He did not feel much refreshed, but when the full light of the day had enveloped the jungle he clambered swiftly down the ruins to the ground and set out once again toward the south, filled with a determination to push on regardless of hunger and fatigue until he had escaped the hideous clutches of this dismal forest, which now seemed to him to have assumed a malignant personality that was endeavouring to foil his efforts and retain him for ever for some sinister purpose of its own. He had come to hate the jungle; he wanted to shout aloud against it the curses that were in his heart. He was impelled to discharge his rifle against it as though it were some creature barring his way to liberty. But he held himself in leash, submerging everything to the desire for escape.

He found that he moved more slowly than he had upon the preceding day. Obstacles were more difficult to surmount, and he was forced to stop more often to rest. These delays galled him; but when he tried to push on more rapidly he often stumbled and fell, and each time he found it more difficult to arise. Then there dawned upon him the realisation that he might not have sufficient strength to reach the edge of the jungle, and for the first time unquestioned fear assailed him.

He sat down upon the ground and, leaning his back against a tree, argued the matter out thoroughly in his own mind. At last his strength of will overcame his fears, so that realisation of the fact that he might not get out that day no longer induced an emotional panic.

"If not to-day, to-morrow," he thought; "if not to-morrow, then the day after. Am I a weakling that I cannot carry on for a few days? Am I to die of starvation in a country abounding in game?"

Physical stamina being so considerably influenced as it is by the condition of the mind, it was with a sense of renewed power that King arose and continued on his way, but imbued now not solely with the desire to escape immediately from the jungle but to wrest from it sustenance and strength that it might be forced to aid him in his escape even though the consummation of his hope might be deferred indefinitely. The psychological effect of this new mental attitude wrought a sudden metamorphosis. He was no longer a hunted fugitive fleeing for his life; he had become in fact a jungle dweller hunting for food and for water. The increasing heat of the advancing day had necessitated inroads upon his scant supply of the latter, yet he still had a few drops left; and these he was determined not to use until he could no longer withstand the tortures of thirst.

He had by now worked out a new and definite plan of procedure; he would work constantly downhill, keeping a sharp look out for game, knowing that eventually he must come to some of the numerous small streams that would ultimately lead him to the Mekong, the large central river that bisects Cambodia on its way to the China Sea; or perchance he might hit upon one of those streams that ran south and emptied into the Tonlé-Sap.

He found it much easier going downhill, and he was glad on this account that he had adopted his present plan. The nature of the country changed a little, too; open spaces were more numerous. Sometimes these flats were marshy, requiring wide detours, and usually they were covered with elephant grass that resembled the cat tails with which he had been familiar as a boy during his summer vacations in the country. He did not like these spaces because they appeared too much the natural habitat of snakes, and he recalled having read somewhere that in a single year there had been sixteen thousand recorded deaths from snake bites in British India alone. This recollection came to him while he was in the centre of a large patch of elephant grass, and consequently he moved very slowly, examining the ground ahead of him carefully at each step. This, of course, necessitated pushing the reeds apart, a slow and laborious procedure; but it also resulted in his moving more quietly; so that when he emerged from the reeds a sight met his eyes that doubtless he would not have seen had he crashed through noisily.

Directly in front of him and maybe fifty paces distant under a great spreading banyan tree lay several wild pigs, all of them comfortably asleep except one old boar, which seemed to be on guard. That King's approach had not been entirely noiseless was evidenced by the fact that the great beast was standing head-on and alert, his ears up-pricked, looking straight at the point at which the man emerged from the elephant grass.

For an instant man and beast stood silently eyeing one another. King saw lying near the boar a half-grown pig, that would make better eating than the tough old tusker. He brought his rifle to his shoulder and fired at the sleeping pig, expecting the remainder of the herd to turn and flee into the jungle; but he had not taken into consideration the violent disposition of the boar. The rest of the herd, awakened with startling suddenness by the unaccustomed report of the rifle, leaped to their feet, stood for an instant in bewilderment, and then turned and disappeared among the undergrowth. Not so the boar. At the crack of the rifle he charged.

There is something rather awe-inspiring in the charge of a wild boar, especially if one happens to be in the path of it, as King was. Perhaps because of his unfamiliarity with the habits of wild boars, the charge was entirely unexpected; and in the brief instant that he had in which to defend himself, he realised that he did not know what was the most vulnerable spot in a boar's anatomy. All that he sensed in that all too short interval were a pair of great flashing tusks, huge jowls, two red-rimmed wicked little eyes, and a stiffly upright tail bearing down upon him with all the velocity and apparently quite the weight of a steam locomotive.

There seemed to be nothing to shoot at but a face. His first shot struck the boar squarely between the eyes and dropped him, but only for an instant. Then he was up again and coming. Giving thanks for a magazine rifle, King pumped three more bullets straight into that terrifying countenance, and to the last one the great beast rolled over against King's feet. None too sure that he had more than stunned him, the man quickly put a bullet through the savage heart.

It had been a close call, and he trembled a little to think what his fate might have been had he been seriously wounded and left there dying in the jungle. Assured that the boar was dead, he went quickly to the pig that had been killed instantly by his first shot. As his knife sank into the flesh, he became suddenly conscious of a change within him. He was moved by urgings that he had never sensed before. He was impelled to bury his teeth in the raw flesh and gorge himself. He realised that this was partially the result of gnawing hunger; but yet it seemed deeper, something primitive and bestial that always had been a part of him but that never before had had occasion to come to the surface. He knew in that brief instant the feeling of the wild beast for its kill. He looked quickly and furtively about to see if there might be any creature bold enough to contest his possession of the fruit of his prowess. He felt the snarling muscles of his upper lip tense and he sensed within him the rumblings of a growl, though no sound passed his lips.

It required a determined effort of will power to refrain from eating the flesh raw, so hungry was he; but he managed to conquer the urge and set about building a fire, though the meal that he finally produced was scarcely more than a compromise, the meat being charred upon the outside and raw within. After he had eaten he felt renewed strength, but now the tortures of thirst assailed him more poignantly than before. His canteen was empty; and though he had passed by stagnant pools of water during the day, he had been able to resist the temptation to drink, realising, as he did, the germs of terrible fever that lurked in these slimy pools.

The next few days constituted a long nightmare of suffering and disappointment. He found his path toward the Mekong barred by impassable swamps that forced him northward over a broken terrain of ravines and ridges that taxed his rapidly waning strength. For some time after leaving the marshes he had seen no water, but upon the third day he came to a pool in the bottom of a ravine. That it was the drinking-hole of wild beasts was evidenced by the multitude of tracks in the muddy bank. The liquid was green and thick, but not for an instant did the man hesitate. Throwing himself upon his belly, he plunged his hands and face into the foul mess and drank. Neither fever nor death could be worse than the pangs of thirst.

Later that day he shot a monkey and, cooking some of the flesh, appeased his hunger; and thus for several days he wandered, shooting an occasional monkey for food and drinking water wherever he found it. He was always conscious of the presence of the great cats, though only upon one or two occasions did he catch fleeting glimpses of them; but at night he heard them moving softly beneath some tree in which he had found precarious sanctuary, where he crouched nursing the hope that no leopard or panther would discover him. Occasionally he saw small herds of wild elephants, and these he always gave a wide berth. He had long given up all hope of escaping from the jungle, and he could not but wonder at

man's tenacity in clinging to life in the face of suffering and
hardship when he knew that at best he was but prolonging
his agony and only temporarily delaying the inevitable.

Seven days and seven nights he had spent in the jungle,
and the last night had been the worst of all. He had dozed
intermittently. The jungle had been full of noises, and he had
seen strange, dim figures passing beneath him. When the
eighth morning broke, he was shivering with cold. His chattering teeth reminded him of castanets. He looked about him
for dancers and was surprised that he saw none. Something
moved through the foliage of the jungle beneath him. It was
yellowish-brown with dark stripes. He called to it and it disappeared. Quite remarkably he ceased to be cold, and instead
his body burned as though consumed by internal fires. The
tree in which he sat swayed dizzily, and then with an effort
he pulled himself together and slipped to the ground. He
found that he was very tired and that he was forced to stop
to rest every few minutes, and sometimes he shook with cold
and again he burned with heat.

It was about noon; the sun was high and the heat terrific.
King lay shivering where he had fallen at the foot of a silk-
cotton tree, against the bole of which he leaned for support.
Far down a jungle aisle he saw an elephant. It was not alone;
there were other things preceding it—things that could not
be in this deserted primeval jungle. He closed his eyes and
shook his head. It was only an hallucination brought on by a
touch of fever, of that he was certain. But when he opened
his eyes again the elephant was still there, and he recognised
the creatures that preceded it as warriors clothed in brass.
They were coming closer. King crawled back into the con-
cealing verdure of the underbrush. His head ached terribly.
There was a buzzing hum in his ears that drowned all other
sounds. The caravan passed within fifty feet of him, but he
heard no sound. There were archers and spear men—brown
men with cuirasses of burnished brass—and then came the
elephant trapped in regal splendour, and in a gorgeous howdah upon its back rode a girl. He saw her profile first, and
then as something attracted her attention she turned her face

full toward him. It was a face of exquisite and exotic beauty, but a sad face with frightened eyes. Her trappings were more gorgeous than the trappings of the elephant. Behind her marched other warriors, but presently all were gone down the aisles of the jungle in spectral silence.

"Weeping queens on misty elephants!" He had read the phrase somewhere in a book. "Gad!" he exclaimed. "What weird tricks fever plays upon one's brain. I could have sworn that what I saw was real."

Slowly he staggered to his feet and pushed on, whither or in what direction he had no idea. It was a blind urge of self-preservation that goaded him forward; to what goal, he did not know; all that he knew was that if he remained where he was he must inevitably perish. Perhaps he would perish anyway, but if he went on, there was a chance. Figures, strange and familiar, passed in jumbled and fantastic procession along the corridors of his mind. Susan Anne Prentice clothed in brass rode upon the back of an elephant. A weeping queen with painted cheeks and rouged lips came and knelt beside him offering him a draft of cold, crystal-clear water from a golden goblet, but when he lifted it to his lips the goblet became a battered canteen from which oozed a slimy green liquid that burned his mouth and nauseated him. Then he saw soldiers in brass who held platters containing steaming sirloin steaks and French-fried potatoes, which changed magically to sherbert, iced tea, and waffles with maple syrup.

"This will never do," thought King. "I am going absolutely daffy. I wonder how long the fever lasts, or how long it takes to finish a fellow."

He was lying upon the ground at the edge of a little clearing partially hid by the tall grass into which he had sunk. Suddenly everything seemed to whirl around in circles, and then the world went black and he lost consciousness. It was very late in the afternoon when he came to; but the fever seemed to have left him, temporarily at least, and his mind was clear.

"This can't go on much longer," he soliloquised. "If I don't find some place pretty soon where I can lie in safety until after the fever has passed entirely, it will be just too bad. I wonder what it feels like to be mauled by a tiger.''

But when he attempted to rise he discovered to his horror that he had not sufficient strength to get to his feet. He still clung to his rifle. He had long since made up his mind that in it lay his principal hope of salvation. Without it, he must go hungry and fall prey to the first beast that attacked him. He knew that if he discarded it and his heavy belt of ammunition he might stagger on a short distance and then, when he fell again, he would be helpless.

As he lay there looking out into the little clearing, speculating upon his fate and trying to estimate the number of hours of life that might remain to him, he saw a strange figure enter the clearing. It was an old man with a straggly white beard growing sparsely upon his chin and upper lip. He wore a long, yellow cloak and a fantastic headdress, above which he carried a red umbrella. He moved slowly, his eyes bent upon the ground.

''Damned fever,'' muttered King, and shut his eyes.

He kept them closed for a minute or two, but when he opened them the old man was still in sight, though by this time he had almost crossed the clearing, and now there was another figure in the picture. From out of the foliage beyond the clearing appeared a savage, snarling face—a great, vicious, yellow-fanged face; yellowish-white and tan with broken markings of dark brown stripes that looked almost black—a hideous head, and yet, at the same time, a gorgeously majestic head. Slowly, silently the great tiger emerged into the clearing, its gaunt, flat-sided body moving sinuously, its yellow-green eyes blazing terribly at the back of the unconscious old man.

''God, how real!'' breathed King. ''I could swear that I really saw them both. Only the impossible figure of that old man with the red parasol could convince me that they are both made of the same material as the spectral elephant, the weeping queen, and the brass-bound soldiers.''

The tiger was creeping rapidly toward the old man. His speed gradually accelerated.

"I can't stand it," cried King, raising his rifle to his shoulder. "They may be only an hallucination—"

There was a short coughing roar as the tiger charged, and at the same instant King squeezed the trigger of his rifle and fainted.

3

The Hunter

Vay Thon, high priest of the temple of Siva in the city of
Lodidhapura, was the source of much anxiety on the part of
the lesser priests, who felt responsible to Siva and the King
for the well-being of Vay Thon. But how might one cope
with the vagaries of a weakness so holy and, at the same
time, so erratic as that which occasionally claimed the am-
nesic Vay Thon? They tried to watch over him at all times,
but it is difficult to maintain constant espionage over one so
holy, whose offices or whose meditations may not lightly be
broken in upon by lesser mortals, even though they be priests
of the great god, Siva.

All was well when Vay Thon confined himself in his meditations to the innermost sanctum of the Holy of Holies; here,
in the safe-keeping of his god, he was isolated from mankind
and safe from danger. But the meditations of Vay Thon were
not always thus securely cloistered. Often he strolled along
the broad terrace beside the mighty temple, where wrapped
in utter forgetfulness of himself and of the world he walked
in silent communion with his god.

With his long, yellow cloak and his red parasol he was
also a familiar figure upon the streets of Lodidhapura. Here
he was often accompanied by lesser priests, who walked in
cuirasses of polished brass, who marched ahead and in the
rear. Of all these symbols of worldly pomp and power, Vay
Thon was entirely unconscious. During those periods that he
was wrapped in the oblivion of meditation and upon the numerous occasions when he had managed to leave the temple
ground unperceived, he had walked through the streets of the

city equally unaware of all that surrounded him. Upon three separate and distinct occasions he had been found wandering in the jungle, and Lodivarman, the King, had threatened to wreak dire punishment upon the lesser priests should harm ever befall Vay Thon during one of these excursions.

It so happened that upon this very day Vay Thon had walked out of the city and into the jungle alone. That he had been able to leave a walled city, the gates of which were heavily guarded by veteran warriors, might have seemed a surprising thing to the citizens of Lodidhapura; but not so to the one familiar with the secret galleries that lay beneath the temple and the palace, through which the ancient builders of Lodidhapura might well have expected to flee the wrath of the downtrodden slaves who comprised 75 per cent of the population. Though times have changed with the passing centuries, the almost forgotten passageways remain. It was through one of these that Vay Thon reached the jungle. He did not know that he was in the jungle. He was as totally oblivious of his surroundings as is one who is wrapped in deep and dreamless sleep.

The last that the lesser priests had seen of Vay Thon was when he had entered the Holy of Holies, which houses the symbol of Siva. As they had noticed a glassy expression in his eyes, they had known that he was entering upon a period of meditation. Therefore, they maintained a watch at the entrance to the chamber, but felt no concern during the passing hours since they knew that Vay Thon was safe. What they did not know of was the loose stone in the flooring of the chamber directly behind the symbol of Siva, or the passageway beneath, which led to a ravine in the jungle beyond the city wall. And so during those hours Vay Thon wandered far into the jungle, and with him, perhaps, walked Siva, the Destroyer.

His rapt meditation, which amounted to almost total unconsciousness of his mundane surroundings, was shattered by a noise of terrific violence such as had never before impinged upon the ears of Vay Thon or any other inhabitant of Lodidhapura. Awakened suddenly as from a deep sleep, the startled priest wheeled about amazed at his surroundings, but more amazed by the sight which greeted his eyes. Wallowing in its own gore scarce three paces behind him lay a great tiger in its death throes; and a little to his right, a wisp of blue smoke rose from some grasses at the edge of the clearing.

When King regained consciousness he was vaguely aware of voices that seemed to be floating in the air about him. The sounds were meaningless, but they conveyed to his fevered brain an assurance of human origin. He opened his eyes. Above him was a brown face. Supporting his head and shoulders he felt the naked flesh of a human arm. His eyes wandered. Standing close was a woman, naked but for a sampot drawn diaperwise between her legs and knotted at the belt. Hiding fearfully behind her was a naked child. The man who supported him spoke to him, but in a language that he could not understand.

From whence had these people come, or were they but figments of his fevered imagination like the old man with the yellow cloak and the red parasol? Were they no more real than the spectral tiger that he had shot at in his delirium? He closed his eyes in an effort to gain control of his senses, but when he opened them again the man and the woman and the child were still there. With a sigh of resignation he gave it up. His throbbing temples were unequal to the demands of sustained thought. He closed his eyes, and his chin dropped upon his breast.

"He is dying," said Che, looking up at the woman.

"Let us take him to our dwelling," replied Kangrey, the woman. "I will watch over him while you lead the holy priest back to Lodidhapura."

As the man lifted King in his arms and turned to carry him away, the American caught a glimpse of an old man in a long, yellow cloak and a strange headdress, who carried above his head a red parasol. The American closed his eyes against the persistent hallucination of his fever. His head swam, and once again he lost consciousness.

King never knew how long he remained unconscious, but

when he next opened his eyes he found himself lying upon a bed of grasses in the interior of a dark retreat which he thought, at first, was a cave. Gradually he discerned the presence of a man, a woman, and a child. He did not remember ever having seen them before. The child was naked, and the man and woman were clothed only in sampots. The woman was ministering to him, forcing a liquid between his lips.

Slowly and sluggishly his mind commenced to function, and at last he recalled them—the creatures of the hallucination that had conjured the image of the old man in the yellow cloak with the red parasol, and the charging tiger that he had dreamed of shooting. Would the fever never leave him? Was he to die thus alone in the sombre jungle tortured by hallucinations that might terminate only with his discovery by a tiger?

But yet how real was the feeling and taste of the liquid that the woman was forcing between his lips. He could even feel the animal warmth of the bare arm that was supporting his head and shoulders. Could any figment of a fever-tortured brain be as realistic as these? Repeatedly he closed his eyes and opened them again, but always the same picture was there before him. He raised one hand weakly and touched the woman's shoulder and face. They seemed real. He was almost convinced that they were when he sank again into unconsciousness.

For days Gordon King hovered between life and death. Kangrey, the woman, ministered to him, utilising the lore of the primitive jungle dweller in the brewing of medicinal potions from the herbs of the forest. Of equal or perhaps greater value were certain incantations which she droned monotonously above him.

Little Uda, the child, was much impressed with all these unusual and remarkable occurrences. The stranger with the pale skin was the first momentous event of his little life. The strange clothing that his parents had removed from their helpless charge thrilled him with awe, as did the rifle, the knife, and the revolver, which he rightfully guessed to be weapons, though he had no more conception of the mechanism of the firearms than did his parents. Uda was indefatigable in his search for the herbs and roots that Kangrey, his mother, required; and when Che returned from the hunt it was always Uda who met him first with a full and complete history of their patient's case brought down to the last minute with infinite attention to details.

At last the fever broke. Though it left King weak and helpless in body, his mind was clear, and he knew at last that the man and the woman and the child were no figments of his imagination. Of course, the old man with the yellow cloak and the red parasol had been but an hallucination of a kind with the charging tiger; but this kindly brown woman, who was nursing him back to health, was real; and his eyes filled as the thanks which he could not voice welled up within his breast.

A day and a night without any return of the fever or hallucination convinced King that the ministration of the kindly natives had rid him of the illness that had nearly killed him, yet he was so weak that he still had little or no hope of ultimate recovery. He had not the strength to raise a hand to his face. It required a real physical effort to turn his head from side to side upon the rough pallet of grasses upon which he lay. He noticed that they never left him alone for long. Either the woman or the child was with him during the day, and all three slept near him upon the floor of their little den at night. In the daytime the woman or the child brushed the flies and other insects from him with a leafy branch and gave him food at frequent intervals. What the food was he did not know except that it was semi-liquid, but now that his fever had passed he was so ravenous that whatever it was they gave him he relished it.

One day when he had been left alone with the little boy longer than usual, the child, possibly tiring of the monotony of brushing insects from the body of the pale one, deserted his post, leaving King alone. King did not care, for much of his time, anyway, was spent in sleep and he had become so accustomed to the insects that they no longer irritated him as they formerly had. He was awakened from a sleep by the feel of a rough hand upon his face. Opening his eyes, he saw a monkey squatting beside him. When King opened his eyes the animal leaped nimbly away, and then the American saw that there were several monkeys in the chamber. They were quite the largest that he had seen in the jungle, and in his helpless condition he knew that they might constitute a real menace to his life. But they did not attack him, nor did they come close to him again; and it soon became evident that their visit was prompted solely by curiosity.

A little later he heard a scraping sound behind him in one corner of the chamber. Having regained his strength during the past few days sufficiently to be able to move his head and hands with comparative ease, he turned his head to see what was going on. The sight that met his eyes would have been highly amusing had it not been fraught with the possibility of such unhappy results.

The monkeys had discovered his weapons and his clothing. All had congregated at the point of interest. They were dragging the things about and chattering excitedly. They seemed to be quarrelling about something; and their chattering and scolding rose in volume until finally one old fellow, who was apparently contesting possession of the rifle with two others, leaped angrily upon them, growling and biting. Instantly the other two relinquished their holds upon the firearm and scurried to a far corner of the chamber; whereupon the victor seized the weapon again and dragged it toward the doorway.

"Hey!" shouted King in the loudest voice he could muster. "Drop that; and get out of here!"

The sound of the human voice seemed to startle the monkeys, but not sufficiently to cause them to relinquish the purpose they had in mind. It is true that they scampered from the chamber, but they gathered up all of King's belongings and took them with them, even to his socks.

King shouted to the boy whom he had heard the parents address as Uda; but when at last the little chap came, breathless and frightened, it was too late to avert or remedy the catastrophe, even if King had been able to explain to Uda what had happened.

The night when she returned, Kangrey found her patient very weak, but she did not guess the cause of it since she could not know that in the mind of the pale one was implanted the conviction that his only hope for eventual escape from the jungle had lain in the protection that the stolen weapons would have afforded him.

The days and nights wore slowly on as gradual convalescence brought returning strength to the sick man. To while away the tedious hours he sought to learn the language of his benefactors; and when, finally, they understood his wish they entered with such spirit into its consummation that he found himself deluged with such a variety of new words that his mind became fogged with information. But eventually some order and understanding came out of the chaos, so that presently he was able to converse with Che and Kangrey and Uda. Thereafter his existence was far less monotonous; but his slow recovery irked and worried him, for it seemed impossible that his strength ever would return. He was so emaciated that it was well for his peace of mind that he had no access to any mirrors.

Yet surely though slowly, his strength was returning. From sitting up with his back against the wall he came at length to standing upon his feet once more; and though he was weak and tottering, it was a beginning; and each day now he found his strength returning more rapidly.

From talking with Che and Kangrey, King had learned the details of the simple life they led. Che was a hunter. Some days he brought back nothing, but as a rule he did not return without adding to the simple larder. The flesh was usually that of a monkey or bird or one of the small rodents that lived in the jungle. Fish he brought, too, and fruit and vegetables and sometimes wild honey.

Che and Kangrey and Uda were equally proficient in making fires with a primitive fire stick, which they twirled between the palms of their hands. Kangrey possessed a single pot in which all food was cooked. It was a brass pot, the inside of which she kept scrupulously polished, using earth and leaves for this purpose.

Che was, indeed, a primitive hunter, armed with a spear, bow and arrows, and a knife. When King explained to him the merits of the firearms that had been stolen by the monkeys, Che sympathised with his guest in their loss; but he promised to equip King with new weapons such as he himself carried; and King expressed his gratitude to the native, though he could not arouse within himself much enthusiasm at the prospect of facing a long trip through this tiger-infested forest armed only with the crude weapons of primitive man, even were he skilled in their use.

As King's strength had returned, he had tried to keep together in his mind the happenings that had immediately preceded his illness, but he always felt that the old man with the yellow cloak and the red parasol and the charging tiger that had fallen to a single shot were figments of a fever-tortured brain. He had never spoken to Che and Kangrey about the hallucination because it seemed silly to do so; yet he found its memory persisting in his mind as a reality rather than an hallucination, so that at last, one evening, he determined to broach the subject, approaching it in a roundabout way.

"Che," he said, "you have lived in the jungle a long while, have you not?"

"Yes," replied the native. "For five years I was a slave in Lodidhapura, but then I escaped, and all the rest of my life I have spent in the jungle."

"Did you ever see an old man wandering in the jungle," continued King, "an old man who wore a long yellow cloak and carried a red parasol?"

"Of course," replied Che, "and you saw him, too. It was Vay Thon, whom you saved from the charge of My Lord the Tiger."

King looked at the native in open-mouthed astonishment. "Have you had a touch of fever too, Che?" he asked

"No," replied the native. "Che is a strong man; he is never ill."

"No," Kangrey said proudly. "Che is a very strong man.

In all the years that I have known him, he has never been ill."

"Did you see this old man with the yellow cloak and the red parasol, Kangrey?" asked King, sceptically.

"Of course I did. Why do you ask?" inquired the woman.

"And you saw me kill the tiger?" demanded the American.

"I did not see you kill him; but I heard a great noise, and I saw him after he had died. There was a little round hole just behind his left ear; and when Che cut him open to see why he died, he found a piece of metal in his brain, the same metal that the walls of the palace of Lodivarman are covered with."

"That is lead," said Che with an air of superiority.

"Then you mean to tell me that this old man and the tiger were real?" demanded King.

"What do you think they were?" asked Che.

"I thought they were of the same stuff as were the other dreams that the fever brought into my brain," replied King.

"No," said Che, "they were not dreams. They were real. And it was good for you and for me and for Vay Thon that you killed the tiger, though how you did it neither Vay Thon nor I can understand."

"It was certainly good for Vay Thon," said King.

"And good for you and for me," insisted Che.

"Why was it so good for us?" asked the American.

"Vay Thon is the high priest of Siva in the city of Lodidhapura. He is very powerful. Only Lodivarman, the King, is more powerful. Vay Thon had wandered far from the city immersed in deep thought. He did not know where he was. He did not know how to return to Lodidhapura. Kangrey and I are runaway slaves of Lodidhapura. Had we been discovered before this happened, we should have been killed; but Vay Thon promised us our freedom if I would lead him back to the city. In gratitude to you for having saved his life he charged Kangrey and me to nurse you back to health and to take care of you. So you see it was good for all of us that you killed the tiger that would have killed Vay Thon."

"And you would not have nursed me back to health, Che, had Vay Thon not exacted the promise from you?" inquired King.

"We are runaway slaves," said the native. "We fear all men, or until Vay Thon promised us our freedom, we did fear all men; and it would have been safer for us to let you die, since you were unknown to us and might have carried word to the soldiers of Lodidhapura and led them to our hiding-place."

For a time King remained in silent thought, wondering, in view of what he had just heard, where the dividing line had lain between reality and hallucination. "Perhaps, then," he said with a smile, "the weeping queen on the misty elephant and the many soldiers in cuirasses of polished brass were real too."

"You saw those?" asked Che.

"Yes," replied King.

"When and where?" demanded the native excitedly.

"It could not have been very long before I saw the high priest and the tiger."

"They are getting close," said Che nervously to Kangrey. "We must search for another hiding-place."

"You forget the promise of Vay Thon," Kangrey reminded him. "We are free now; we are no longer slaves."

"I had forgotten," said Che. "I am not yet accustomed to freedom, and perhaps I think, too, that possibly Vay Thon may forget."

"I do not think so," said the woman. "Lodivarman might forget, but not Vay Thon, for Vay Thon is a good man. Every one in Lodidhapura said so."

"You really believe that I saw an elephant, a queen, and soldiers?" demanded King.

"Why not?" asked Che.

"There are such things in the jungle?" inquired the young man.

"Of course," said Kangrey.

"And this city of Lodidhapura?" demanded King. "I have never heard of it before. Is that close beside the jungle?"

"It is in the jungle," said Che.

King shook his head. "It is strange," he said. "I wandered through the jungle for days and never saw signs of a human being or a human habitation."

"There are many things in the jungle which men do not always see," replied Che. "There are the Nagas and the Yeacks. You may be glad that you did not see them."

"What are the Nagas and the Yeacks?" asked King.

"The Nagas are the Cobra people," replied Che. "They live in a great palace upon a mountain and are very powerful. They have seven heads and can change themselves into any form of creature that they desire. They are workers of magic. It is said that Lodivarman's principal wife is the queen of the Nagas and that she changed herself into the form of a beautiful woman that she might rule directly over the mortals as well as the gods. But I do not believe that, because no one, not even a Naga, would choose to be the queen of a leper. But the Yeacks are most to be feared because they do not live far away upon a mountain-top, but are everywhere in the jungle."

"What are they like?" asked King.

"They are horrible Ogres who live upon human flesh," replied Che.

"Have you ever seen them?" asked King.

"Of course not," replied the native. "Only he who is about to be devoured sees them."

Gordon King listened with polite attention to the folk tales of Che and Kangrey, but he knew that they were only legends of a kind with the fabulous city of Lodidhapura and its Leper King, Lodivarman. He was somewhat at a loss to account for Vay Thon, the high priest, but he decided finally that the old man was an eccentric hermit who had come into the jungle to live and that to him might be attributed many of the fabulous tales that Che and Kangrey narrated so glibly. That his two friends were runaway slaves from the fabulous city of Lodidhapura, King doubted, attributing their story to the desire of primitive minds to inject a strain of romance into their otherwise monotonous lives.

As King's strength returned rapidly, he insisted more and more upon getting out into the open. He was anxious to accompany Che upon his hunting trips, but the native insisted that he was not yet sufficiently strong. So the American had to content himself with remaining with Kangrey and Uda at home, where he practised using the weapons that Che had made for him, which consisted of a bow and arrow and a short, heavy javelin-like spear. Thanks to the training of his college days, King was proficient in the use of the latter; and he practised assiduously with his bow and arrows until his marksmanship aroused the admiring applause of even Kangrey, who considered Che the best bowman in the world, to whose expert proficiency no other mortal might hope to attain.

The dwelling of Che and Kangrey and Uda was in an ancient Khmer ruin and consisted of a small room which had withstood the march of the centuries—a room that was peculiarly suited to the requirements of the little jungle family since it had but a single entrance, a small aperture that could be effectually blocked at night with a flat slab of stone against the depredations of marauding cats.

Their existence was as simple and primitive as might have been that of the first man; yet there was inherent in it an undeniable charm that King felt in spite of the monotony and his anxiety to escape from the jungle.

Che knew nothing but the jungle and the fabulous city of Lodidhapura. It is difficult for us to conceive of an endless infinity of space, but Che could imagine an endless jungle. The question of limitation did not enter his mind and, therefore, did not confuse him. To him, the world was a jungle. When King realised this, he knew, too, that it was hopeless to expect Che to attempt to lead him out of a jungle that he believed had no end.

For some time King had been making short excursions into the jungle in search of game while he repeatedly sought to impress upon Che that he was strong enough to accompany the native upon his hunts; but he was met with so many excuses that he at last awoke to the fact that Che did not want him along; and so the American determined to set out by himself upon a prolonged and determined effort to prove his efficiency. He left one morning after Che had departed, turning his steps in a different direction from that taken by the native. He was determined to bring back something to demonstrate his prowess to Che, but though he moved silently through the jungle, keeping the sharpest look out, he saw no sign of game of any description; and having had past experience of the ease with which one might become lost in the jungle, he turned back at last empty-handed.

During his long convalescence King had had an opportunity to consider many things, and one of them had been his humiliating lack of jungle craft. He knew, therefore, that he must mark the trail in some way if he were to hope to return to the dwelling of Che and Kangrey. He could not blaze the trees with his knife on a hunting excursion since the noise would unquestionably frighten away the game, and so he invented several other ways of marking the trail—sticking twigs in the rough bark of trees that he passed, scraping the ground with the sharp point of his javelin, and placing three twigs in the form of an arrow, pointing backward along the trail over which he had come. Accordingly, he had little difficulty to-day in back-tracking along the way to the home of Che.

Practising jungle craft necessitated moving as noiselessly as possible, and so it was that he came as silently as might a hunting cat to the edge of the ruin where lay the dwelling of his friend. As King came within sight of the familiar entrance, a scene met his eyes that froze his blood and brought his heart into his throat. In the small clearing that Che had made, little Uda was at play. He was digging with a sharp stick in the leafy mould of the ground, while watching him at the edge of the clearing crouched a great panther.

King saw the beast gradually drawing its hind feet well beneath its body as it prepared to charge.

4

Fou-tan

Returning early from a successful hunt, Che approached the clearing. He, too, moved silently, for thus he always moved through the jungle. Along a forest aisle he could see the clearing before he reached it. He saw Uda digging among the dry leaves, which made a rustling sound that would have drowned the noise of the approach of even a less careful jungle animal than Che. The father smiled as his eyes rested upon his first-born, but in the same instant the smile froze to an expression of horror as he saw a panther leap into the clearing.

Kangrey, emerging at that moment from their gloomy dwelling, saw it too, and screamed as she rushed forward barehanded, impelled by the mother instinct to protect its young. And then, all in the same brief instant, Che saw a heavy javelin streak lightning-like from the jungle. He saw the panther crumple in its charge, and as he ran forward he saw the pale one leap into the clearing and snatch Uda into his arms.

Che, realising, as had King, the fury of a wounded panther, rushed upon the scene with ready spear as the pale one tossed Uda to Kangrey and turned again to face the great cat. But there was no necessity for the vicious thrust with which Che drove his spear into the carcass of the beast, for the panther was already dead.

For a moment they stood in silence, looking down upon the kill—four primitive jungle people, naked but for sampots. It was King's first experience of a thrill of the primitive hunter. He trembled a little, but that was reaction to the fear that he had felt for the life of little Uda.

"It is a large panther," said Che simply.

"Only a strong man could have slain it thus," said Kangrey. "Only Che could thus have slain with a single cast so great a panther."

"It was not the spear of Che. It was the spear of the pale one that laid low the prince of darkness," said Che.

Kangrey looked her astonishment and would not be convinced until she had examined the spear that protruded from beneath the left shoulder of the great cat. "This, then, is the reward that Vay Thon said would be ours if we befriended the pale one," she declared.

Uda said nothing, but, squirming from his mother's arms, he ran to the side of the dead panther and belaboured it with his little stick.

The next day Che invited King to accompany him upon his hunt. When after a hard day they returned empty-handed, King was convinced that in the search for small game a lone hunter would have greater chances for success. In the morning, therefore, he announced that he would hunt alone in another part of the jungle, and Che agreed with him that this plan would be better.

Marking his trail as he had before, King hunted an unfamiliar territory. The forest appeared more open. There was less underbrush; and he had discovered what appeared to be a broad elephant trail, along which he moved with far greater speed than he had ever been able to attain before in his wanderings through this empire of trees and underbrush.

He had no luck in his hunting; and when he had about determined that it was time to turn back, his ears caught an unfamiliar sound. What it was he did not know. There was a peculiar metallic ring and other sounds that might have been human voices at a distance.

"Perhaps," soliloquised King, "I am about to see the Nagas or the Yeacks."

The sound was steadily approaching; and as he had learned enough from his intercourse with Che and Kangrey to know that no friendly creatures might be encountered in the jungle, he drew to one side of the elephant trail and concealed himself behind some shrubbery.

He had not waited long when he saw the authors of the sounds approaching. Suddenly he felt his head. It did not seem over-hot. As he had upon other similar occasions, he closed his eyes tightly and then opened them again, but still the vision persisted—a vision of brown-skinned soldiers in burnished brass cuirasses over leather jerkins that fell midway between their hips and their knees, with heavy sandals on their feet, strange helmets on their heads, and armed with swords and spears and bows and arrows.

They came on talking among themselves, and as they passed close to King he discovered that they spoke the same language that he had learned from Che and Kangrey. Evidently the men were arguing with their leader, who wanted to go on, while the majority of his followers seemed in favour of turning back.

"We shall have to spend the night in the jungle as it is," said one. "If we go on much farther, we shall have to spend two nights in the jungle. Only a fool would choose to lair with My Lord the Tiger."

They had stopped now almost opposite King, so that he could clearly overhear all that passed between them. The man in charge appeared to be a petty officer with little real authority, for instead of issuing orders he argued and pleaded.

"It is well enough for you to insist upon turning back," he said, "since if we return to the city without the apsaras you expect that I alone shall be punished; but let me tell you that, if you force me to turn back, the entire truth will be made known and you will share in any punishment that may be inflicted upon me."

"If we cannot find her, we cannot find her," grumbled one of the men. "Are we to remain in the jungle the rest of our lives searching for a runaway apsaras?"

"I would as lief face My Lord the Tiger in the jungle for the rest of my life," replied the petty officer, "as face Lodivarman if we return without the girl."

"What Vama says is true," said another. "Lodivarman, the King, will not be interested in our reason for returning empty-handed. Should we return to the city to-morrow without the girl and Vama charged that we had forced him to turn back, Lodivarman, if he were in ill-humour, as he usually is, would have us all put to death; but if we remain away for many days and then return with a story of many hardships and dangers he will know that we did all that might be expected of brave warriors, and thus the anger of Lodivarman might be assuaged."

"At last," commented Vama, "you are commencing to talk like intelligent and civilised men. Come, now, and let us resume the search."

As they moved away King heard one of the men suggest that they find a safe and comfortable camp site where they might remain for a sufficient length of time to impress upon the King the verity of the story that they would relate to him. He waited only until they were out of sight before he arose from his place of concealment, for he was much concerned with the fact that they were proceeding in the general direction of the dwelling of Che and Kangrey. King was much mystified by what he had seen. He knew that these soldiers were no children of a fevered brain. They were flesh and blood warriors and for that reason a far greater mystery than any of the creatures he had seen in his delirium, since they could not be accounted for by any process of intelligent reasoning. His judgment told him that there were no warriors in this uninhabited jungle and certainly none with the archaic accoutrements and weapons that he had seen. It might be reasonable to expect to meet such types in an extravaganza of the stage or screen; and, doubtless, centuries ago warriors such as these patrolled this very spot which the jungle and the tiger and the elephant had long since reclaimed.

He recalled the stories that his guide had told him of the ghosts of the ancient Khmers, which roamed through the sombre aisles of the forest. He remembered the other soldiers that he had seen and the girl with the frightened eyes that rode upon the great elephant, and the final result was a questioning of his own sanity. Since he knew that a fever, such as the one through which he had passed, might easily affect one's brain either temporarily or permanently, he was troubled and not a little frightened as he made his way in the direction of the dwelling of Che and Kangrey. But the fact that he took a circuitous route that he might avoid the warriors indicated that either he was quite crazy or, at least, that he was temporising with his madness.

" 'Weeping queens on misty elephants!' " he soliloquised. " 'Warriors in brass!' 'A mystery of the Orient.' Perhaps after all there are ghosts. There has been enough evidence accumulated during historic times to prove that the materialisation of disembodied spirits may have occurred upon countless occasions. That I never saw a ghost is not necessarily conclusive evidence that they do not exist. There are many strange things in the Orient that the western mind cannot grasp. Perhaps, after all, I have seen ghosts; but if so, they certainly were thoroughly materialised, even to the dirt on their legs and the sweat on their faces. I suppose I shall have to admit that they are ghosts, since I know that no soldiers like them exist in the flesh anywhere in the world."

As King moved silently through the jungle, he presented an even more anachronistic figure than had the soldiers in brass; for they, at least, personified an era of civilisation and advancement, while King, to all outward appearances, was almost at the dawn of human evolution—a primitive hunter, naked but for a sampot of leopard skin and rude sandals fashioned by Kangrey because the soles of his feet, innocent of the callouses that shod hers and Che's, had rendered him almost helpless in the jungle without this protection. His skin was brown from exposure to the sun, and his hair had grown thick and shaggy. That he was smooth-shaven was the result of chance. He had always made it a habit, since he had taken up the study of medicine and surgery, to carry a safety razor blade with him, for what possible emergency he could not himself have explained. It was merely an idiosyncrasy, and it had so chanced that among several other things that the monkeys had dropped from his pockets and scattered in the jungle the razor blade had been recovered by little Uda along with a silver pencil and a handful of French francs.

He moved through the jungle with all the assurance of a man who has known no other life, so quickly does humankind adapt itself to environment. Already his ears and his nostrils had become inured to their surroundings to such an extent, at least, as to permit them to identify and classify easily and quickly the more familiar sounds and odours of the jungle. Familiarity had induced increasing self-assurance, which had now reached a point that made him feel he might soon safely set out in search of civilisation. However, to-day his mind was not on this thing; it was still engaged in an endeavour to solve the puzzle of the brass-bound warriors. But presently the baffling contemplation of this matter was rudely interrupted by a patch of buff coat and black stripes of which he caught a momentary, fleeting glimpse between the boles of two trees ahead of him.

A species of unreasoning terror that had formerly seized him each time that he had glimpsed the terrifying lord of the jungle had gradually passed away as he had come to recognise the fact that every tiger that he saw was not bent upon his destruction and that nine times out of ten it would try to get out of his way. Of course, it is the tenth tiger that one must always reckon with; but where trees are numerous and a man's eyes and ears and nose are alert, even the tenth tiger may usually be circumvented.

So now King did not alter his course, though he had seen the tiger directly ahead of him. It would be time enough to think of retreat when he found that the temper and intentions of the tiger warranted it, and, further, it was better to keep the brute in sight than to feel that perhaps he had circled and was creeping up behind one. It was, therefore, because of this that King pushed on a little more rapidly; and soon he was rewarded by another glimpse of the great carnivore and of something else, which presented a tableau that froze his blood.

Beyond the tiger and facing it stood a girl. Her wide eyes were glassy with terror. She stood as one in a trance, frozen to the spot, while toward her the great cat crept. She was a slender girl, garbed as fantastically as had been the soldiers that had passed him in the jungle shortly before; but her gorgeous garments were soiled and torn, and even at a distance King could see that her face and arms were scratched and bleeding. In the instant that his eyes alighted upon her he sensed something strangely familiar about her. It was a sudden, wholly unaccountable impression that somewhere he had seen this girl before; but it was only a passing impression, for his whole mind now was occupied with her terrifying predicament.

To save her from the terrible death creeping slowly upon her seemed beyond the realms of possibility, and yet King knew that he must make the attempt. He recognised instantly that his only hope lay in distracting the attention of the tiger. If he could centre the interest of the brute upon himself, perhaps the girl might escape.

He shouted, and the tiger wheeled about. "Run!" he cried to the girl. "Quick! Make for a tree!"

As he spoke, King was running forward. His heavy spear was ready in his hand, but yet it was a mad chance to take. Perhaps he forgot himself and his own danger, thinking only of the girl. The tiger glanced back at the girl, who, obeying King's direction, had run quickly to a nearby tree into which she was trying to scramble, badly hampered by the long skirt that enveloped her.

For only an instant did the tiger hesitate. His short and ugly temper was fully aroused now in the face of this rude interruption of his plan. With a savage snarl and then the short coughing roars with which King was all too familiar, he wheeled and sprang toward the man in long, easy bounds. Twelve to fifteen feet he covered in a single leap. Flight was futile. There was nothing that King could do but stand his ground and pit his puny spear against this awful engine of destruction.

In that brief instant there was pictured upon the screen of his memory a tree-girt athletic field. He saw young men in shirts and shorts throwing javelins. He saw himself among them. It was his turn now. His arm went back. He recalled how he had put every ounce of muscle, weight, and science into that throw. He recalled the friendly congratulations that followed it, for every one knew without waiting for the official verdict that he had broken a world's record.

Again his arm flew back. To-day there was more at stake than a world's record, but the man did not lose his nerve. Timed to the fraction of an instant, backed by the last ounce of his weight and his skill and his great strength, the spear met the tiger in mid-leap; full in the chest it struck him. King leaped to one side and ran for a tree, his single, frail hope lying in the possibility that the great beast might be even momentarily disabled.

He did not waste the energy or the time even to glance behind him. If the tiger were able to overtake him, it must be totally a matter of indifference to King whether the great brute seized him from behind or in front—he had led his ace and he did not have another.

No fangs or talons rent his flesh as King scrambled to the safety of the nearest tree. It was not without a sense of considerable surprise that he found himself safely ensconced in his leafy sanctuary, for from the instant that the tiger had turned upon him in its venomous charge he had counted himself already as good as dead.

Now that he had an opportunity to look about him, he saw the tiger struggling in its death throes upon the very spot where it had anticipated wreaking its vengeance upon the rash man-thing that had dared to question its right to the possession of its intended prey; and a little to the right of the dying beast the American saw the girl crouching in the branches of a tree. Together they watched the death throes of the great cat; and when at last the man was convinced that the beast was dead, he leaped lightly to the ground and approached the tree among the branches of which the girl had sought safety.

That she was still filled with terror was apparent in the strained and frightened expression upon her face. "Go away!'' she cried. ''The soldiers of Lodivarman, the King, are here; and if you harm me they will kill you.''

King smiled. ''You are inconsistent,'' he said, ''in invoking the protection of the soldiers from whom you are trying to escape; but you need not fear me. I shall not harm you.''

''Who are you?'' she demanded.

''I am a hunter who dwells in the jungle,'' replied King. ''I am the protector of high priests and weeping queens, or so, at least, I seem to be.''

''High priests? Weeping queens? What do you mean?''

''I have saved Vay Thon, the high priest, from My Lord the Tiger,'' replied King; ''and now I have saved you.''

''But I am no queen and I am not weeping,'' replied the girl.

''Do not disillusion me,'' insisted King. ''I contend that you are a queen, whether you weep or smile. I should not be surprised to learn that you are the queen of the Nagas. Nothing would surprise me in this jungle of anachronism, hallucination, and impossibility.''

''Help me down from the tree,'' said the girl. ''Perhaps you are mad, but you seem quite harmless.''

''Be assured, your majesty, that I shall not harm you,'' replied King, ''for presently I am sure there will emerge from nowhere ten thousand elephants and a hundred thousand warriors in shining brass to succour and defend you. Nothing seems impossible after what I have witnessed; but come, let me touch you; let me assure myself that I am not again the victim of a pernicious fever.''

''May Siva, who protected me from My Lord the Tiger a moment ago, protect me also from this madman!''

''Pardon me,'' said King. ''I did not catch what you said.''

''I am afraid,'' said the girl.

''You need not be afraid of me,'' King assured her; ''and if you want your soldiers I believe that I can find them for you; but if I am not mistaken, I believe that you are more afraid of them than you are of me.''

''What do you know of that?'' demanded she.

''I overheard their conversation while they halted near

me," replied the American, "and I learned that they are hunting for you to take you back to someone from whom you escaped. Come, I will help you down. You may trust me."

He raised his hands toward her, and after a moment's hesitation she slipped into his arms and he lowered her to the ground.

"I must trust you," she said. "There is no other way, for I could not remain for ever in the tree; and then, too, even though you seem mad there is something about you that makes me feel that I am safe with you."

As he felt her soft, lithe body momentarily in his arms, King knew that this was no tenuous spirit of a dream. For an instant her small hand touched his shoulder, her warm breath fanned his cheek, and her firm, young breasts were pressed against his naked body. Then she stepped back and surveyed him.

"What manner of man are you?" she demanded. "You are neither Khmer nor slave. Your colour is not the colour of any man that I have ever seen, nor are your features those of the people of my race. Perhaps you are a reincarnation of one of those ancients of whom our legends tell us; or perhaps you are a Naga who has taken the form of man for some dire purpose of your own."

"Perhaps I am a Yeack," suggested King.

"No," she said quite seriously, "I am sure you are not a Yeack, for it is reported that they are most hideous, while you, though not like any man I have ever seen, are handsome."

"I am neither Yeack nor Naga," replied King.

"Then perhaps you are from Lodidhapura—one of the creatures of Lodivarman."

"No," replied the man. "I have never been to Lodidhapura. I have never seen the King, Lodivarman, and, as a matter of fact, I have always doubted their existence."

The girl's dark eyes regarded him steadily. "I cannot believe that," she said, "for it is unconceivable that there should be anyone in the world who has not heard of Lodidhapura and Lodivarman."

"I come from a far country," explained King, "where there are millions of people who never heard of the Khmers."

"Impossible!" she cried.

"But nevertheless quite true," he insisted.

"From what country do you come?" she asked.

"From America."

"I never heard of such a country."

"Then you should be able to understand that I may never have heard of Lodidhapura," said the man.

For a moment the girl was silent, evidently pondering the logic of his statement. "Perhaps you are right," she said finally. "It may be that there are other cities within the jungle of which we have never heard. But tell me—you risked your life to save mine—why did you do that?"

"What else might I have done?" he asked.

"You might have run away and saved yourself."

King smiled, but he made no reply. He was wondering if there existed any man who could have run away and left one so beautiful and so helpless to the mercies of My Lord the Tiger.

"You are very brave," she continued presently. "What is your name?"

"Gordon King."

"Gordon King," she repeated in a soft, caressing voice. "That is a nice name, but it is not like any name that I have heard before."

"And what is your name?" asked King.

"I am called Fou-tan," she said, and she eyed him intently, as though she would note if the name made any impression upon him.

King thought Fou-tan a pretty name, but it seemed banal to say so. He was appraising her small, delicate features, her beautiful eyes and her soft brown skin. They recalled to him the weeping queen upon the misty elephant that he had seen in his delirium, and once again there arose within him doubts as to his sanity. "Tell me," he said suddenly. "Did you ever ride through the jungle on a great elephant escorted by soldiers in brass?"

"Yes," she said.

"And you say that you are from Lodidhapura?" he continued.

"I have just come from there," she replied.

"Did you ever hear of a priest called Vay Thon?"

"He is the high priest of Siva in the city of Lodidhapura," she replied.

King shook his head in perplexity. "It is hard to know," he murmured, "where dreams end and reality begins."

"I do not understand you," she said, her brows knit in perplexity.

"Perhaps I do not understand myself," he admitted.

"You are a strange man," said Fou-tan. "I do not know whether to fear you or trust you. You are not like any other man I have ever known. What do you intend to do with me?"

"Perhaps I had better take you back to the dwelling of Che and Kangrey," he said, "and then to-morrow Che can guide you back to Lodidhapura."

"But I do not wish to return to Lodidhapura," said the girl.

"Why not?" demanded King.

"Listen, Gordon King, and I shall tell you," said Fou-tan.

5

The Capture

"Let us sit down upon this fallen tree," said Fou-tan, "and I shall tell you why I do not wish to return to Lodidhapura."

As they seated themselves, King became acutely conscious of the marked physical attraction that this girl of a forgotten age exercised over him. Every movement of her lithe body, every gesture of her graceful arms and hands, each changing expression of her beautiful face and eyes were provocative. She radiated magnetism. He sensed it in the reaction of his skin, his eyes, his nostrils. It was as though ages of careful selection had produced her for the purpose of arousing in man the desire of possession, and yet there enveloped her a divine halo of chastity that aroused within his breast the protective instinct that governs the attitude of a normal man toward a woman that Fate has thrown into his keeping. Never in his life had King been similarly attracted to any woman.

"Why do you look at me so?" she inquired suddenly.

"Forgive me," said King simply. "Go on with your story."

"I am from Pnom Dhek," said Fou-tan, "where Beng Kher is king. Pnom Dhek is a greater city than Lodidhapura; Beng Kher is a mightier king than Lodivarman.

"Bharata Rahon desired me. He wished to take me to wife. I pleaded with my father the—I pleaded with my father not to give me in marriage to Bharata Rahon; but he told me that I did not know my own mind, that I only thought that I did not like Bharata Rahon, that he would make me a good husband, and that after we were married I should be happy.

51

"I knew that I must do something to convince my father that my mind and soul sincerely revolted at the thought of mating with Bharata Rahon, and so I conceived the idea of running away and going out into the jungle that I might prove that I preferred death to the man my father had chosen for me.

"I did not want to die. I wanted them to come and find me very quickly, and when night came I was terrified. I climbed into a tree where I crouched in terror. I heard My Lord the Tiger pass beneath in the darkness of the night, and my fear was so great that I thought that I should faint and fall into his clutches; yet when day came again I was still convinced that I would rather lie in the arms of My Lord the Tiger than in those of Bharata Rahon, who is a loathsome man whose very name I detest.

"Yet I moved back in the direction of Pnom Dhek, or rather I thought that I did, though now I am certain that I went in the opposite direction. I hoped that searchers sent out by my father would find me, for I did not wish to return of my own volition to Pnom Dhek.

"The day dragged on and I met no searchers, and once again I became terrified, for I knew that I was lost in the jungle. Then I heard the heavy tread of an elephant and the clank of arms and men's voices, and I was filled with relief and gratitude, for I thought at last that the searchers were about to find me.

"But when the warriors came within view, I saw that they wore the armour of Lodivarman. I was terrified and tried to escape them, but they had seen me and they pursued me. Easily they overtook me, and great was their joy when they looked upon me.

" 'Lodivarman will reward us handsomely,' they cried, 'when he sees that which we have brought to him from Pnom Dhek.'

"So they placed me in the howdah upon the elephant's back and took me through the jungle to Lodidhapura, where I was immediately taken into the presence of Lodivarman.

"Oh, Gordon King, that was a terrible moment. I was

terrified when I found myself so close to the leper king of Lodidhapura. He is covered with great sores, where leprosy is devouring him. That day he was ugly and indifferent. He scarcely looked at me, but ordered that I should be taken to the quarters of the apsarases, and so I became a dancing girl at the court of the leper king.

"Not in a thousand years, Gordon King, could I explain to you what I suffered each time that we came before Lodivarman to dance. Each sore upon his repulsive body seemed to reach out to seize and contaminate me. It was with the utmost difficulty that, half fainting, I went through the ritual of the dance.

"I tried to hide my face from him, for I knew that I was beautiful and I knew the fate of beautiful women in the court of Lodivarman.

"But at last, one day, I realised that he had noticed me. I saw his dead eyes following me about. We were dancing in the great hall where he holds his court. Lodivarman was seated upon his throne. The lead-covered walls of the great apartment were gorgeous with paintings and with hangings. Beneath our feet were the polished flagstones of the floor, but they seemed softer to me than the heart of Lodivarman.

"At last the dance was done, and we were permitted to retire to our apartments. Presently there came to me a captain of the King's household, resplendent in his gorgeous trappings.

" 'The King has looked upon you,' said he, 'and would honour you as befits your beauty.'

" 'It is sufficient honour,' I replied, 'to dance in the palace of Lodivarman.'

" 'You are about to receive a more signal manifestation of the King's honour,' he replied.

" 'I am satisifed as I am,' I said.

" 'It is not for you to choose, Fou-tan,' replied the messenger. 'The King has chosen you as his newest concubine. Rejoice, therefore, in the knowledge that some day you may become queen.'

"I could have fainted at the very horror of the suggestion.

What could I do? I must gain time. I thought of suicide, but I am young, and I do not wish to die. 'When must I come?' I asked.

" 'You will be given time to prepare yourself,' replied the messenger. 'For three days the women will bathe and anoint your body, and upon the fourth day you will be conducted to the King.'

"Four days! In four days I must find some way in which to escape the horrid fate to which my beauty had condemned me. 'Go!' I said. 'Leave me in peace for the four days that remain to me of even a semblance of happiness in life.'

"The messenger, grinning, withdrew, and I threw myself upon my pallet and burst into tears. That night the apsarases were to dance in the moonlight in the courtyard before the temple of Siva; and though they would have insisted that my preparation for the honour that was to be bestowed upon me should commence at once, I begged that I might once more, and for the last time, join with my companions in honouring Siva, the Destroyer.

"It was a dark night. The flares that illumined the court-yard cast a wavering light in which exaggerated shadows of the apsarases danced grotesquely. In the dance I wore a mask, and my position was at the extreme left of the last line of apsarases. I was close to the line of spectators that encircled the courtyard, and in some of the movements of the dance I came quite close enough to touch them. This was what I had hoped for.

"All the time that I was dancing I was perfecting in my mind the details of a plan that had occurred to me earlier in the day. The intricate series of postures and steps, with which I had been familiar since childhood, required of me but little mental concentration. I went through them mechanically, my thoughts wholly centred upon the mad scheme that I had conceived. I knew that at one point in the dance the attention of all the spectators would be focused upon a single apsaras, whose position was in the centre of the first line, and when this moment arrived I stepped quickly into the line of spectators.

"Those in my immediate vicinity noticed me, but to these I explained that I was ill and was making my way back to the temple. A little awed by my close presence, they let me pass unmolested, for in the estimation of the people the persons of the apsarases are almost holy.

"Behind the last line of the audience rose a low wall that surrounds the temple courtyard. Surmounting it at intervals rise the beautifully carved stone figures of the seven-headed cobra—emblem of the Royal Nagas. Deep were the shadows between them; and while all eyes were fixed upon the leading apsaras, I clambered quickly to the top of the low wall, where for a moment I hid in the shadow of a great Naga. Below me, black, mysterious, terrifying, lay the dark waters of the moat, beneath the surface of which lived the crocodiles placed there by the King to guard the Holy of Holies. Upon the opposite side the level of the water was but a few inches below the surface of the broad avenue that leads to the stables where the King's elephants are kept. The avenues were deserted, for all who dwelt within the walls of the royal enclosure were watching the dance of the apsarases.

"To Brahma, to Vishnu, and to Siva I breathed a prayer, and then I slid as quietly as possible down into the terrifying waters of the moat. Quickly I struck out for the opposite side, every instant expecting to feel the hideous jaws of a crocodile close upon me; but my prayers had been heard, and I reached the avenue in safety.

"I was forced to climb two more walls before I could escape from the royal enclosure and from the city. My wet and bedraggled costume was torn, and my hands and face were scratched and bleeding before I succeeded.

"At last I was in the jungle, confronted by danger more deadly, yet far less horrible, than that from which I had escaped. How I survived that night and this day I do not know. And now the end would have come but for you, Gordon King."

As King gazed at the sensitive face and delicately moulded figure of the girl beside him, he marvelled at the courage and strength of will, seemingly so out of proportion to the frail temple that housed them, that had sustained her in the conception and execution of an adventure that might have taxed the courage and stamina of a warrior. "You are a brave girl, Fou-tan," he said.

"The daughter of my father could not be less," she replied simply.

"You are a daughter of whom any father might be proud," said King, "but if we are to save you for him we had better be thinking about getting to the dwelling of Che and Kangrey before night falls."

"Who are these people?" asked Fou-tan. "Perhaps they will return me to Lodidhapura for the reward that Lodivarman will pay."

"You need have no fear on that score," replied King. "They are honest people, runaway slaves from Lodidhapura. They have been kind to me, and they will be kind to you."

"And if they are not, you will protect me," said Fou-tan with a tone of finality that evidenced the confidence which she already felt in the dependability and integrity of her new-found friend.

As they set out in the direction of Che's dwelling, it became apparent to King immediately that Fou-tan was tired almost to the point of exhaustion. Will-power and nerve had sustained her so far; but now, with the discovery of someone to whom she might transfer the responsibility of her safety, the reaction had come; and he often found it necessary to assist and support her over the rough places of the trail. She was small and light, and where the going was exceptionally bad he lifted her in his arms and carried her as he might have a child.

"You are strong, Gordon King," she said once as he carried her thus. Her soft arms were around his neck, her lips were very close to his.

"I must need be strong," he said. But if she sensed his meaning she gave no evidence of it. Her eyes closed wearily and her little head dropped to his shoulder. He carried her thus for a long way, though the trail beneath his feet was smooth and hard.

Vama and his warriors had halted in a little glade where

there was water. While two of them hunted in the forest for meat for their supper, the others lay stretched out upon the ground in that silence which is induced by hunger and fatigue. Presently Vama sat up alert. His ears had caught the sound of the approach of something through the jungle.

"Kau and Tchek are returning from the hunt," whispered one of the warriors who lay near him and who, also, had heard the noise.

"They did not go in that direction," replied Vama in a low tone. Then signalling his warriors to silence, he ordered them to conceal themselves from view.

The sound, already close when they had first heard it, approached steadily; and they did not have long to wait ere a warrior, naked but for a sampot, stepped into view, and in his arms was the runaway apsaras whom they sought. Elated, Vama leaped from his place of concealment, calling to his men to follow him.

At sight of them King turned to escape, but he knew that he could make no speed while burdened with the girl. She, however, had seen the soldiers and slipped quickly from his arms. "We are lost!" she cried.

"Run!" cried King as he snatched a handful of arrows from his quiver and fitted one to his bow. "Stand back!" he cried to the warriors. But they only moved steadily forward. His bow-string twanged, and one of Lodivarman's brass-bound warriors sank to earth, an arrow through his throat. The others hesitated. They did not dare to cast their spears or loose their bolts for fear of injuring the girl.

Slowly King, with Fou-tan behind him, backed away into the jungle from which he had appeared. At the last instant he sped another arrow, which rattled harmlessly from the cuirass of Vama. Then, knowing that he could not fire upon them from the foliage, the soldiers rushed forward, while King continued to fall back slowly with Fou-tan, another arrow fitted to his bow.

Kau and Tchek had made a great circle in their hunting. With their arrows they had brought down three monkeys, and now they were returning to camp. They had almost arrived when they heard voices and the twang of a bow-string, and then they saw, directly ahead of them, a man and a girl crashing through the foliage of the jungle toward them. Instantly, by her dishevelled costume, they recognised the apsaras and guessed from the attitude of the two that they were backing away from Vama and his fellows.

Kau was a powerful, a courageous, and a resourceful man. Instantly he grasped the situation and instantly he acted. Leaping forward, he threw both his sinewy arms around Gordon King, pinning the other's arms to his body; while Tchek, following the example of his companion, seized Fou-tan. Almost immediately Vama and the others were upon the scene. An instant later Gordon King was disarmed, and his wrists were bound behind him; then the soldiers of Lodivarman dragged the captives back to their camping place.

Vama was tremendously elated. Now he would not have to make up any lies to appease the wrath of his king but could return to Lodidhapura in triumph, bearing not only the apsaras for whom he had been dispatched, but another prisoner as well.

King thought that they might make quick work of him in revenge for the soldier he had killed, but they did not appear to hold that against him at all. They questioned him at some length while they cooked their supper of monkey meat over a number of tiny fires; but as what he told them of another country far beyond their jungle was quite beyond their grasp, they naturally believed that he lied and insisted that he came from Pnom Dhek and that he was a runaway slave.

They were all quite content with the happy outcome of their assignment; and so, looking forward to their return to Lodidhapura on the morrow, they were inclined to be generous in their treatment of their prisoners, giving them meat to eat and water to drink. Their attitude toward Fou-tan was one of respectful awe. They knew that she was destined to become one of the King's favourites, and it might prove ill for them, indeed, should they offer her any hurt or affront. Since their treatment of Gordon King, however, was not dictated by any such consideration, it was fortunate, indeed, for him that they were in a good humour.

Regardless, however, of the respectful attention shown her, Fou-tan was immersed in melancholy. A few moments before, she had foreseen escape and counted return to her native city almost an accomplished fact; now, once again, she was in the clutches of the soldiers of Lodivarman, while simultaneously she had brought disaster and, doubtless, death to the man who had befriended her.

"Oh, Gordon King," she said, "my heart is unstrung; my soul is filled with terror and consumed by horror, for not only must I return to the hideous fate from which I had escaped, but you must go to Lodidhapura to slavery or to death."

"We are not in Lodidhapura yet," whispered King. "Perhaps we shall escape."

The girl shook her head. "There is no hope," she said. "I shall go to the arms of Lodivarman, and you—"

"And I?" he asked.

"Slaves fight with other slaves and with wild beasts for the entertainment of Lodivarman and his court," she replied.

"We must escape then," said King. "Perhaps we shall die in the attempt, but in any event death awaits me and worse than death awaits you."

"What you command I shall do, Gordon King," replied Fou-tan.

But it did not appear that there was to be much opportunity for escape that night. After King had eaten they bound his wrists behind his back again and also bound his ankles together securely, while two warriors remained constantly with the girl; the others, their simple meal completed, stripped the armour and weapons from their fallen comrade and laid him upon a thick bed of dry wood that they had gathered. Upon him, then, they piled a great quantity of limbs and branches, of twigs and dry grasses; and when night fell they lighted their weird funeral pyre, which was to answer its other dual purpose as a beast fire to protect them from the prowling carnivores. To King it was a gruesome sight, but neither Fou-tan nor the other Khmers seemed to be affected by it. The men gathered much wood and placed it near at hand that the fire might be kept burning during the night.

The flames leaped high, lighting the boles of the trees about them and the foliage arching above. The shadows rose and fell and twisted and writhed. Beyond the limits of the firelight was utter darkness, silence, mystery. King felt himself in an inverted cauldron of flame in which a human body was being consumed.

The warriors lay about, laughing and talking. Their reminiscences were brutal and cruel. Their jokes and stories were broad and obscene. But there was an undercurrent of rough kindness and loyalty to one another that they appeared to be endeavoring to conceal as though they were ashamed of such soft emotion. They were soldiers. Transplanted to the camps of modern Europe, given a modern uniform and a modern language, their campfire conversation would have been the same. Soldiers do not change. One played upon a little musical instrument that resembled a Jew's harp. Two were gambling with what appeared to be very similar to modern dice, and all that they said was so interlarded with strange and terrible oaths that the American could scarcely follow the thread of their thought. Soldiers do not change.

Vama came presently and squatted down near King and Fou-tan. "Do all the men in this far country of which you tell me go naked?" he demanded.

"No," replied the American. "When I had become lost in the jungle I was stricken with fever, and while I was sick the monkeys came and stole my clothing and my weapons."

"You live alone in the jungle?" asked Vama.

King thought quickly; he thought of Che and Kangrey and their fear of the soldiers in brass. "Yes," he said.

"Are you not afraid of My Lord the Tiger?" inquired Vama.

"I am watchful and I avoid him," replied the American.

"You do well to do so," said Vama, "for even with spear and arrows no lone man is a match for the great beast."

"But Gordon King is," said Fou-tan proudly.

Vama smiled. "The apsaras has been in the jungle but a night and a day," he reminded her. "How can she know so much about this man unless, as I suspect, he is, indeed, from Pnom Dhek?"

"He is not from Pnom Dhek," retorted Fou-tan. "And I know that he is a match for My Lord the Tiger because this day I saw him slay the beast with a single spear-cast."

Vama looked questioningly at King.

"It was only a matter of good fortune," said King.

"But you did it nevertheless," insisted Fou-tan.

"You killed a tiger with a single cast of your spear?" demanded Vama.

"As the beast charged him," said Fou-tan.

"That is, indeed, a marvellous feat," said Vama, with a soldier's ungrudging admiration for the bravery or prowess of another. "Lodivarman shall hear of this. A hunter of such spirit shall not go unrecognised in Lodidhapura. I can also bear witness that you are no mean bowman," added Vama, nodding toward the blazing funeral pyre. Then he arose and walked to the spot where King's weapons had been deposited. Picking up the spear he examined it closely. "By Siva!" he ejaculated. "The blood is scarcely dry upon it. Such a cast! You drove it a full two feet into the carcass of My Lord the Tiger."

"Straight through the heart," said Fou-tan.

The other soldiers had been listening to the conversation. It was noticeable immediately that their attitude toward King changed instantly, and thereafter they treated him with friendliness tinged by respect. However, they did not abate their watchfulness over him, but rather were increasingly careful to see that he was given no opportunity to escape, nor to have his hands free for any length of time.

Early the next morning, after a meagre breakfast, Vama set out with his detachment and his prisoners in the direction of Lodidhapura, leaving the funeral fire still blazing as it eagerly licked at a new supply of fuel.

The route they selected to Lodidhapura passed by chance, close to the spot where King had slain the tiger; and here, in the partially devoured carcass of the great beast, the soldiers of Lodivarman found concrete substantiation of Fou-tan's story.

6

※

The Leper King

It was late in the afternoon when the party emerged suddenly from the jungle at the edge of a great clearing. King voiced an involuntary exclamation of astonishment as he saw at a distance the walls and towers of a splendid city.

"Lodidhapura," said Fou-tan; "accursed city!" There was fear in her voice, and she trembled as she pressed closer to the American.

While King had long since become convinced that Lodidhapura had an actual existence of greater reality than legend or fever-wrought hallucination, yet he had been in no way prepared for the reality. A collection of nippa-thatched huts had comprised the extent of his mental picture of Lodidhapura, and now, as the reality burst suddenly upon him, he was dumbfounded.

Temples and palaces of stone reared their solid masses against the sky. Mighty towers, elaborately carved, rose in stately grandeur high over all. There were nippa-thatched huts as well, but these clustered close against the city's walls and were so overshadowed by the majestic mass of masonry beyond them that they affected the picture as slightly as might the bushes growing at its foot determine the grandeur of a mountain.

In the foreground were level fields in which laboured men and women, naked mostly, but for sampots—the nippa-thatched huts were their dwellings. They were the labourers, the descendants of slaves—Chams and Annamese—that the ancient, warlike Khmers had brought back from many a victory in the days when their power and their civilisation were the greatest upon earth.

From the edge of the jungle, at the point where the party had emerged, a broad avenue led toward one of the gates of the city, toward which Vama was conducting them. To his right, at a distance, King could see what appeared to be another avenue leading to another gate—an avenue which seemed to be more heavily travelled than that upon which they had entered. There were many people on foot, some approaching the city, others leaving it. At a distance they looked small, but he could distinguish them and also what appeared to be bullock carts moving slowly among the pedestrians.

Presently, at the far end of this distant avenue, he saw the great bulks of elephants; in a long column they entered the highway from the jungle and approached the city. They seemed to move in an endless procession, two abreast, hundreds of them, he thought. Never before had King seen so many elephants.

"Look!" he cried to Fou-tan. "There must be a circus coming to town."

"The King's elephants," explained Fou-tan, unimpressed.

"Why does he have so many?" asked King.

"A king without elephants would be no king," replied the girl. "They proclaim to all men the king's wealth and power. When he makes war, his soldiers go into battle upon them and fight from their backs, for those are the war elephants of Lodivarman."

"There must be hundreds of them," commented the American.

"There are thousands," said Fou-tan.

"And against whom does Lodivarman make war?"

"Against Pnom Dhek."

"Only against Pnom Dhek?" inquired King.

"Yes, only against Pnom Dhek."

"Why does he not make war elsewhere? Has he no other enemies?"

"Against whom else might he make war?" demanded Fou-tan. "There are only Pnom Dhek and Lodidhapura in all the world."

"Well, that does rather restrict him now, doesn't it?" admitted King.

For a moment they were silent. Then the girl spoke. "Gordon King," she said in that soft, caressing voice that the man found so agreeable, that often he had sought for means to lure her into conversation. "Gordon King, soon we shall see one another no more."

The American frowned. He did not like to think of that. He had tried to put it out of his mind and to imagine that by some chance they would be allowed to be together after they reached Lodidhapura, for he had found Fou-tan a cheery and pleasant companion even when her hour was darkest. Why, she was the only friend he had! Certainly they would not deny him the right to see her. From what he had gleaned during his conversation with Vama and the other warriors, King had become hopeful that Lodivarman would not treat him entirely as a prisoner or an enemy, but might give him the opportunity to serve the King as a soldier. Fou-tan had rather encouraged this hope too, for she knew that it was not at all improbable of realisation.

"Why do you say that?" demanded King. "Why shall we not see one another again?"

"Would you be sad, Gordon King, if you did not see Fou-tan any more?" she asked.

The man hesitated before he replied, as though weighing in his mind a problem that he had never before been called upon to consider; and as he hesitated a strange, hurt look came into the eyes of the girl.

"It is unthinkable, Fou-tan," he said at last, and the great brown eyes of the little apsaras softened and tears rose in them. "We have been such good friends," he added.

"Yes," she said. "We have known each other but a very short time, and yet we seem such good friends that it is almost as though we had known each other always."

"But why should we not see one another again?" he demanded once more.

"Lodivarman may punish me for running away, and there is only one punishment that would satisfy his pride in such an event and that is death; but if he forgives me, as he doubtless will, because of my youth and my great beauty and his desire for me, then I shall be taken into the King's palace and no more then might you see me than if I were dead. So you see, either way, the result is the same."

"I shall see you again, Fou-tan," said the man.

She shook her head. "I like to hear you say it, even though I know that it cannot be."

"You shall see, Fou-tan. If we both live I shall find a way to see you; and, too, I shall find a way to take you out of the palace of the King and back to Pnom Dhek."

She looked up at him with earnest eyes, full of confidence and admiration. "When I hear you say it," she said, "the impossible seems almost possible."

"Cling to the hope, Fou-tan," he told her; "and when we are separated, know always that my every thought will be centered upon the means to reach you and take you away."

"That will help me to cling to life until the last horrible minute, beyond which there can be no hope and beyond which I will not go."

"What do you mean, Fou-tan?" There had been that in her voice which frightened him.

"I can live in the palace of the King with hope until again the King sends for me, and then—"

"And then?"

"And then—death."

"No, Fou-tan, you must not say that. You must not think it."

"What else could there be—after?" she demanded. "He is a leper!" The utter horror in her voice and expression, as her lips formed the word, aroused to its fullest the protective instinct of the man. He wanted to throw an arm about her, to soothe and reassure her; but his wrists were bound together behind him, and he could only move on dumbly at her side toward the great, carved gate of Lodidhapura.

The sentry at the gate halted Vama and his party, though his greeting, following his formal challenge, indicated that he was well aware of the identity of all but King, a fact which impressed the American as indicative of the excellent military discipline that obtained in this remote domain of the leper king.

Summoned by the sentry, the captain of the gate came from his quarters within the massive towers that flanked the gateway to Lodidhapura. He was a young man, resplendent in trappings of gold and blue and yellow. His burnished cuirass and his helmet were of the precious metal, but his weapons were stern and lethal.

"Who comes?" he demanded.

"Vama of the King's guard, with the apsaras from Pnom Dhek, who ran away into the jungle, and a warrior from a far country whom we took prisoner," replied the leader of the detachment.

"You have done well, Vama," said the officer, as his eyes quickly appraised the two captives. "Enter and go at once to the palace of the King, for such were his orders in the event that you returned successful from your quest."

The streets of Lodidhapura, beyond the gate, were filled with citizens and slaves. Tiny shops with wide awnings lined the street through which Vama's captives were conducted. Merchants in long robes and ornate headdresses presided over booths where were displayed a bewildering variety of merchandise, including pottery, silver and gold ornaments, rugs, stuffs, incense, weapons, and armour.

Men and women of high rank, beneath gorgeous parasols borne by almost naked slaves, bartered at the booths for the wares displayed; high-hatted priests moved slowly through the throng, while burly soldiers elbowed their way roughly along the avenue. Many turned to note the escort and its prisoners, and the sight of Fou-tan elicited a wealth of ejaculation and many queries; but to all such Vama, fully aware of his importance, turned a deaf ear.

As they approached the centre of Lodidhapura, King was amazed by the evident wealth of the city, by the goods displayed in the innumerable shops, and by the grandeur of the architecture. The ornate carvings that covered the façades of the great buildings, the splendour of the buildings themselves, filled him with awe; and when at last the party halted before the palace of Lodivarman, the American was staggered by the magnificence which confronted him.

They had been conducted through a great park that lay below, and to the east of the stately temple of Siva, which dominated the entire city of Lodidhapura. Great trees and gorgeous shrubbery shadowed winding avenues that were flanked by statues and columns of magnificent, though sometimes barbaric, design; and then the palace of the King had burst suddenly upon his astonished gaze—a splendid building embellished from foundation to loftiest tower with tile of the most brilliant colouring and fanciful design.

Before the entrance to the palace of Lodivarman stood a guard of fifty warriors. No brass-bound soldiers these, resplendent in shining cuirasses of burnished gold, whose haughty demeanour bespoke their exalted position and the high responsibility that devolved upon them.

Gordon King had difficulty in convincing himself of the reality of the scene. Again and again his sane Yankee head assured him that no such things might exist in the jungles of Cambodia and that he still was the victim of the hallucinations of high fever; but when the officer at the gate had interrogated Vama and presently commands were received to conduct the entire party to the presence of Lodivarman, and still the hallucination persisted in all its conclusiveness, he resigned himself to the actualities that confronted him and would have accepted as real whatever grotesque or impossible occurrences or figures might have impinged themselves upon his perceptive faculties.

Escorted by a detachment of the golden warriors of Lodivarman, the entire city was conducted through long corridors toward the centre of the palace and at last, after a wait before massive doors, was ushered into a great hall, at the far end of which a number of people were seated upon a raised dais. Upon the floor of the chamber were many men in gorgeous raiment—priests, courtiers, and soldiers. One of the latter, resplendent in rich trappings, received them and conducted them toward the far end of the chamber, where they were halted before the dais.

King saw seated upon a great throne an emaciated man, upon every exposed portion of whose body were ugly and repulsive sores. To his right and below him were sombre men in rich garb, and to his left a score of sad-eyed girls and women. This, then, was Lodivarman, the Leper King of Lodidhapura! The American felt an inward revulsion at the mere sight of this repulsive creature and simultaneously understood the horror that Fou-tan had evinced at the thought of personal contact with the leper into whose clutches fate had delivered her.

Before Lodivarman knelt a slave, bearing a great salver of food, into which the King continually dipped with his long-nailed fingers. He ate almost constantly during the audience, and as King was brought nearer he saw that the delicacies intended to tempt the palate of a king were naught but lowly mushrooms.

"Who are these?" demanded Lodivarman, his dead eyes resting coldly on the prisoners.

"Vama, the commander of ten," replied the officer addressed, "who has returned from his mission, to the honour of the King, with the apsaras for whom he was dispatched and a strange warrior whom he took prisoner."

"Fou-tan of Pnom Dhek," demanded Lodivarman, "why did you seek to escape the honour for which I had destined you?"

"Great King," replied the girl, "my heart is still in the land of my sire. I would have returned to Pnom Dhek, for I longed for the father and the friends whom I love and who love me."

"A pardonable desire," commented Lodivarman, "and this time thy transgression shall be overlooked, but beware a repetition. You are destined to the high honour of the favour of Lodivarman. See that hereafter, until death, thou dost merit it.''

Fou-tan, trembling, curtsied low; and Lodivarman turned his cold, fishy eyes upon Gordon King. ''And what manner of man bringeth you before the King now?'' he asked.

''A strange warrior from some far country, Glorious King,'' replied Vama.

''A runaway slave from Pnom Dhek more likely,'' commented Lodivarman.

''Even as I thought, Resplendent Son of Heaven,'' answered Vama; ''but his deeds are such as to leave no belief that he be either a slave or the son of slaves.''

''What deeds?'' demanded the King.

''He faced my detachment single-handed, and with a lone shaft he slew one of the best of the King's bowmen.''

''Is that all?'' asked Lodivarman. ''A mere freak of Fate may account for that.''

''No, Brother of the Gods,'' replied Vama. ''There is more.''

''And what is it? Hasten, I cannot spend the whole evening in idle audience over a slave.''

''With a single spear-cast he slew My Lord the Tiger,'' cried Vama.

''And you saw this?''

''Fou-tan saw it, and all of us saw the carcass of the tiger the following morning. O King, he drove his spear a full two feet into the breast of the tiger as the great beast charged. He is a marvellous warrior, and Vama is proud to have brought such a one to serve in the ranks of the army of Lodivarman.''

For a while Lodivarman was silent, his dead eyes upon King, while he helped himself from time to time to the tender-cooked mushrooms with which the slave tempted him.

''With a single cast he slew My Lord the Tiger?'' demanded Lodivarman of Fou-tan.

''It is even so, Great King,'' replied the girl.

''How came he to do it? Surely no sane man would tempt the great beast unless in dire predicament.''

"He did it to save me, upon whom the tiger was preparing to spring."

"So I am doubly indebted to this stranger," said Lodivarman. "And what gift would suit your appetite for reward?" demanded the King.

"I desire no reward," replied the American, "only that you will permit Fou-tan to return to her beloved Pnom Dhek."

"You do not ask much!" cried Lodivarman. "I like your ways. You shall not be destroyed, but instead you shall serve me in the palace guards; such a spear-man should prove worth his weight in gold. As for your request, remember that Fou-tan belongs to Lodivarman, the King, and so may no longer be the subject of any conversation, upon pain of death. Take him to the quarters of the guard!" he directed one of his officers, nodding at King, "and see that he is well cared for, trained and armed."

"Yes, most magnificent of kings," replied the man addressed.

"Take the girl to the quarters of the women and look to it that she does not again escape," commanded Lodivarman, with a gesture that dismissed them all.

As he was escorted from the audience chamber through one exit, King saw Fou-tan led away toward another. Her eyes were turned back toward him, and in them was a haunting suggestion of grief and hopelessness that cut him to the heart.

"Good-by, Gordon King!" she called to him.

"Until we meet again, Fou-tan," he replied.

"You will not meet again," said the officer who was escorting him, as he hustled the American from the chamber.

The barracks to which King was assigned stood a considerable distance in the rear of the palace, not far from the stables in which were housed the King's elephants, yet, like the latter, within the grounds of the royal enclosure. The long, low buildings that housed the soldiers of Lodivarman's royal guard were plastered inside and out with mud and thatched with palm fronds. Along either wall upon the hard-packed dirt floors were pallets of straw, where the common soldiers were bedded down like horses. A space of some four feet in width by seven in length was allotted to each man, and into the wall above his pallet pegs had been driven upon which he might hang his weapons and his clothing, a cooking-pot, and a vessel for water. Along the centres of the buildings was a clear space about eight feet wide, forming an aisle in which soldiers might be formed for inspection. Just beneath the eaves was an open space running the full length of both walls, giving ample ventilation but very little light to the interior of the barracks. The doors were at either end of the buildings.

The building to which King was escorted was about two hundred feet long and housed a hundred men. It was but one of a number of similar structures, which he later learned were placed at strategic positions just inside the wall of the royal enclosure, where five thousand men-at-arms were constantly maintained.

At Vama's request King was assigned to his unit of ten to replace the soldier that he had slain in the jungle, and thus the American took up his life in the unit of ten, with Kau and Tchek and Vama and the others with whom he was already acquainted as his companions.

From a naked jungle hunter to a soldier of a Khmer king, he had crossed in a single step long ages of evolution, and yet he was still a thousand years from the era into which he had been born.

7

❦

A Soldier of the Guard

The lives of private soldiers of the royal guard of a Khmer king were far from thrilling. Their most important assignment was to guard duty, which fell to the lot of each soldier once in every four days. There were drills daily, both upon foot and upon elephants, and there were numerous parades and ceremonies.

Aside from the care of their own weapons they were called upon for no manual labour, such work being attended to by slaves. Once a week the straw which formed their pallets was hauled away upon bullock-carts to the elephants' stables, where it was used to bed down the great pachyderms, and fresh straw was brought to the barracks.

Their leisure, of which they usually had a little at various times during the day, the soldiers utilised in gossiping or gambling, or listening to the story-tellers, certain of whom were freely admitted to the royal grounds. Many were the stories to which King listened—stories of ancient power and stories of kings who owned a million slaves and a hundred thousand elephants; stories of Kambu, the mythical founder of the Khmer race; of Yacovarman, the king of glory; and of Jayavarman VIII, the last of the great kings. Interwoven throughout all the fabric of these hoary tales were the Nagas and the Yeacks, those ever-recurring mythological figures that he had met in the folk-lore of the people beyond the jungle, in the dark dwelling of Che and Kangrey, and now in the shadow of the palace of the great King, Lodivarman.

Or when there were no story-tellers, or he tired of listening to the idle gossip of his fellows, or became bored by their endless games of chance, King would sit in silence, meditating upon the past and seeking an answer to the riddle of the future. Recollection of his distant home and friends always raised a vision of Susan Anne Prentice—home and friends and Susan Anne—they were all one; they constituted his past and beckoned him into the future. It seemed difficult to think of life without home and friends and Susan Anne when he thought of them, but always the same little figure rose in front of them, clear and distinct, as they faded slowly out of the picture: sad eyes in which there yet dwelt a wealth of inherent happiness and mirth, a piquant face, and gleaming teeth behind red lips. Always his thoughts, no matter how far they roamed, returned to this dainty flower of girlhood, and then his brows would contract and his jaws clench and he speculated upon her fate and chafed and fretted because of his inability to succour her.

And one day as he sat meditating thus he saw a strange figure approaching across the barracks yard. "Ye gods!" he exclaimed, almost audibly; "one by one my dreams are coming true! If it isn't the old bird with the red umbrella that I saw just before Che and Kangrey rescued me, I'll eat my shirt."

King had had considerable difficulty in differentiating between the fantastic figures of his fever-induced hallucinations and the realities of his weird experiences in the jungle, so that though Che and Kangrey had insisted that there had been an old man with a long yellow robe and a red umbrella and although King had believed them, yet it was with somewhat of a shock that he recognised the reality. As Vay Thon passed among the soldiers, they arose to their feet and bowed low before him, evincing the awe and reverence in which they held him. He passed them with nodding head and mumbled benediction, gazing intently at each face as though he sought some particular warrior.

Seeing that the others rose and bowed before the high priest, King did likewise; and when Vay Thon's eyes fell upon him they lighted with recognition. "It is you, my son," he said. "Do you recall me?"

"You are Vay Thon, the high priest of Siva," replied the American.

"He whom you saved from My Lord the Tiger," replied the priest.

"An obligation which you fully discharged when you commanded Che and Kangrey to nurse me back to life."

"An obligation that I may never fully discharge," replied Vay Thon; "and because of this I came to search for you, that I may offer you proof of my undying gratitude."

"How did you know that I was here?" asked King.

"I have talked with Fou-tan," replied Vay Thon, "and when she had described the warrior who had rescued her, I knew at once that it must be you."

"You have seen Fou-tan and talked with her?" asked King. The high priest nodded.

"And she is well—and safe?" demanded King.

"Her body is well, but her heart is sick," replied the high priest; "but she is safe—those who find favour in the eyes of the King are always safe, while the King's favour lasts."

"Has she—has he—"

"I understand what you would ask, my son," said Vay Thon. "Lodivarman has not yet sent for her."

"But he will," cried King.

"To-night, I think," said Vay Thon.

The anguish in the young man's eyes would have been apparent to one of far less intelligence and discernment than Vay Thon. He laid his hand in compassion upon the shoulder of the American. "If I could help you, my son, I would," he said; "but in such matters kings may not be crossed even by gods."

"Where is she?" asked King.

"She is in the King's house," replied Vay Thon, pointing toward a wing of the palace that was visible from where they stood.

For a long moment the eyes of the American, lighted by determination and by a complexity of other fires that burned within him, remained riveted upon the house of the King.

Vay Thon, the high priest of Siva, was old and wise and

shrewd. "I read your heart, my son," he said, "and my heart goes out in sympathy to yours, but what you plan is impossible of execution; it would but lead to torture and to death."

"In what room is she in the house of the King?" demanded the American.

Vay Thon shook his head sadly. "Forget this madness," he said. "It can lead but to the grave. I am your friend and I would help you, but I would be no friend were I to encourage you in the mad venture that I can only too well guess is forming in your mind. I owe you my life; and always shall I stand ready to aid you in any way that lies within my power, except in this. And now, farewell; and may the gods cause you to forget your sorrow."

As Vay Thon turned and walked slowly back in the direction of the temple, Gordon King stood gazing at the house of Lodivarman; forgotten were Vay Thon; forgotten were his wise words of counsel. King seemed hypnotised; a single figure filled the retina of his mind's eye—a tiny figure, yet it crowded out all else—through walls of tile and lead he saw it crouching in despair in the house of the King.

The afternoon was drawing to a close. The warriors who were to relieve the palace guard at sundown were already buckling on their brass cuirasses, straightening their leather tunics, adjusting their helmets, polishing weapons until they glistened even in the dark interior of the barracks.

Gordon King was recalled to his surroundings by two tardy warriors who were hastening to accoutre themselves for guard duty; and in that instant was born the mad scheme that, without the slightest consideration, he was to attempt to put into execution.

Turning quickly, he overtook the men just before they entered the barracks and touched one of them upon the shoulder. "May I have a word with you?" he asked.

"I have no time. I am already late," replied the warrior.

"I shall be quick, then," replied King. "Let me take your place on the guard to-night, and I will give you all of my next pay."

Instantly the man was all suspicion. "That is a strange

request," he said. "Most warriors would pay to be relieved of guard duty. What is your purpose?"

"There is a certain slave girl attached to the house of the King, and to-night she will be looking for a certain warrior." And the American nudged the other in the ribs and gave him a sly wink.

The warrior's face relaxed into a grin. "It might go hard with us if we were caught," he said; "but, by Siva, three months' pay is not to be considered lightly. Quick! Get into your harness, while I explain the matter to the others of the ten. But be sure that you do not say anything about the pay, for if they knew that, each would want his share."

"You are doing it for friendship," said King with a laugh, as he hastened into the interior of the barracks. As he hurriedly adjusted his cuirass and helmet, the warrior whose place he was to take was explaining the matter to the other members of the ten, who received it with rough laughter and broad jokes.

At first the petty officer in command of the ten positively forbade the exchange, and it was necessary for King to promise him a month's pay before he, at last, reluctantly acceded. "But remember," he admonished them, "I know nothing of it, for no such thing may be done with my knowledge."

As the ten marched toward the house of the King, the American's excitement increased, though outwardly he was calm. Just what he was going to do and just how he was going to execute it, the man could not know, because he had no idea as to what obstacles would present themselves, or, upon the other hand, what good fortune might lie in store for him. He fully appreciated that his proposed action was unwise, ill-considered, and almost definitely doomed to defeat; but could he have turned back he would not have done so.

Presently they were halted at the King's house, a little to one side of the main entrance and before a low doorway. Other contingents of the guard were arriving from other barracks, while members of the old guard emerged from the low doorway and were formed for the brief ceremony that marked the changes of the guard.

Immediately following the ceremony a number of the new guard were told off to relieve the sentries upon their posts about the grounds and within the interior of the palace, and King happened to be among these. As he was marched away he could not help but wonder what post Fate would select for him, though wherever it should be he was determined that he would find the means for gaining access to the interior of the palace.

The detail of the guard was first marched to the far end of the wing, and here a sentry was relieved who paced back and forth in front of a tiny doorway, shadowed by trees and shrubbery. King thought that this would have been an excellent post; but it did not fall to him; and as they continued on about the wing of the palace, relieving sentry after sentry, he began to fear that he was not going to be posted at all; and, indeed, the detail traversed the outside of the entire wing, and still the American had been assigned no post. And then they came at last before the ornate entrance to the King's house, where ten men were detached from the detail to relieve those posted at this important spot.

All the sentries hitherto relieved were then marched away, and King found himself one of five who had not as yet been posted. These, to the astonishment and gratification of the American, were marched into the palace. Three were detailed to posts in the long entrance corridor, while King and the other remaining warrior were marched to the doorway of a large and luxuriously furnished apartment. At one end of the chamber, raised slightly above the floor level, was a dais covered with gorgeous rugs. Upon it stood a low table laid with a service of solid gold, with bowls of fruit and sweetmeats, several massive golden jugs, and ornately carved goblets. Behind the table was a pile of pillows covered with rich stuff, and over all a canopy of cloth of gold. On the floor of the chamber, below the dais, was a long table, similarly though not so richly laid; and this was entirely surrounded by rich cushions.

On either side of the doorway, facing the interior of the room, stood King and his fellow warrior, two bronze statues cuirassed in burnished brass. For five minutes they stood there thus facing the empty chamber; and then a door at the far side opened, and a file of slaves entered, some twenty-five or thirty in all. Two of these took their places at opposite ends of the dais back of the table and the pillows, standing erect with arms folded and eyes staring straight to the front. The other slaves took similar positions at intervals behind the long table on the main floor and faced the dais. Between the long table and the dais and facing the latter stood a richly garbed individual whom King mentally classified as a sort of major-domo.

Again there was a wait of several minutes, during which no one spoke or moved. Then, through the doorway which King and his fellow guarded, a party of men entered the chamber. Some were warriors, cuirassed and helmeted in gold, while others were garbed in long robes of vivid hues, richly embroidered. A number of these wore fantastic head-dresses, several of which were over two feet in height.

These banquet guests formed in little groups behind the long table, engaged in low-toned conversation. There was no laughter now and they spoke scarcely above a whisper. It was as though a pall of gloom had enveloped them the instant they entered the gorgeously appointed chamber. Almost immediately an arras at the rear of the dais was drawn aside, revealing a warrior of the guard, who sounded a fanfare upon a golden trumpet. As the last note died away, the slaves in the chamber prostrated themselves, pressing their foreheads to the floor, while the guests kneeled with bowed heads; and then Lodivarman, the Leper King of Lodidhapura, came slowly through the opening at the rear of the dais. Only the trumpeter and the two guards at the door remained standing as Lodivarman advanced and seated himself upon the pillows behind his table. For a moment he looked about the apartment through his dull eyes, and then, apparently satisfied, he struck his palms together a single time.

Immediately all in the apartment arose to their feet. The major-domo bowed low three times before the King. Each of the guests did the same, and then, in silence, took their places at the banquet table. When all had been seated, Lodivarman struck his palms together a second time; and immediately the slaves stepped forward upon noiseless feet and commenced to serve the viands and pour the wine. A third time Lodivarman gave the signal, upon which the guests relaxed and entered into low-voiced conversation.

From his post at the entrance-way, Gordon King noticed the bountiful array of food upon the long banquet table. Only a few of the articles did he recognise, but it was evident that fruit and vegetables and meat were there in abundance. The largest bowl upon the little table of the King was filled with mushrooms, aside from which there was little else upon Lodivarman's table other than fruit, sweetmeats, and wine. From what he had previously seen of Lodivarman and from the gossip that he had heard in the barracks he was aware that this monarch was so addicted to the use of mushrooms that the eating of them had become a fixed habit with him almost to the exclusion of proper and natural food, and his taste for them was so inordinate that he had long since ordained them royal food, forbidden under pain of death to all save the King.

As the tiresome meal progressed, the banqueters carried on their forced and perfunctory conversation, while Lodivarman sat silent and morose, his attention divided between his mushrooms and his wine. As King watched he could not but compare this meal with formal dinners he had attended in New York and Washington, and he sympathised with the banqueters in the hall of Lodivarman, because he knew that they were suffering the same boredom that he had once endured, but with the advantage that they did not have to appear to be happy and gay.

Presently Lodivarman made a sign to the major-domo, who clapped his hands twice; and immediately all eyes turned to a doorway at one side of the chamber, through which there now filed a company of apsarases. About the hips the girls wore girdles of virgin gold, which supported skirts that fell to within a few inches of their ankles. From their hips two stiff-pointed panels of cloth bowed outward, falling almost to the floor. Above the hips their bodies were naked, except for rich armlets and necklaces. Their headdresses were fantastic contrivances that resembled ornate candelabra, heavy ear-rings fell to their shoulders, and above their bare feet were anklets of precious metal. A few wore masks of hideous design, but the painted lips and cheeks and darkened eyes of most of them were pretty; but there was one among them who was gorgeous in her loveliness. As the eyes of Gordon King fell upon her face, he felt his heart quicken, for she was Fou-tan. She had not seen him when she entered; and now she danced with her back toward him, a dance that consisted of strange postures of the feet and legs, the hips, the arms and hands and heads of the little dancers. As they went through the slow steps of the dance, they bent their fingers, their hands, and their arms into such unnatural positions that Gordon King marvelled, not only upon the long hours and days of practice that must have been necessary for them to perfect themselves, but also upon the mentality of an audience that could find entertainment in such a combination of beauty and grotesqueness. That the dance was ritualistic and had some hidden religious significance was the only explanation that he could place upon it, yet even so he realised that it was fully as artistic and beautiful and intelligent as much of the so-called aesthetic dancing that he had been compelled to endure in modern America and Europe.

There were twenty apsarases taking part in the dance, but King saw only one—a lithe and beautiful figure that moved faultlessly through the long sequences of intricate and difficult posturing. Mad scheme after mad scheme passed through his mind as he sought for some plan whereby he might take advantage of their proximity to effect her release from the palace of the King, but each one must needs be discarded in the light of sober reflection. He must wait, but while he waited he planned and hoped.

As the long dance drew to a close, Gordon King saw Lodivarman beckon to the major-domo to him and whisper briefly to that functionary; and as the apsarases were withdrawing from the room, the man hastened after them and touched Fou-tan upon the shoulder. He spoke to her, and King could see the girl shrink. Lodivarman clapped his hands three times, and again the slaves prostrated themselves and the guests kneeled; while Lodivarman rose to his feet and walked slowly from the chamber through the same doorway by which he had entered. Immediately after he was gone the guests arose and left the chamber, apparently only too glad to be released from the ordeal of a state banquet. The slaves began to gather up the dishes and bear them away, while the major-domo led Fou-tan across the chamber, up on to the royal dais and bowed her into the doorway through which Lodivarman had disappeared.

Gordon King could scarce restrain himself as the full import of what he had just witnessed revealed itself to his tortured mind. Inclination prompted him to run across the chamber and follow Lodivarman and Fou-tan through that doorway of mystery, but again sane judgment interposed.

With the passing of the King and the guests, the American's fellow guardsman had relaxed. He no longer stood in statuesque immobility, but lounged carelessly against the wall watching the slaves bearing away the trays of unfinished food. "We should enjoy that more than the guests seemed to," he said to King, nodding toward the viands.

"Yes," replied the American, his mind upon other matters.

"I have stood guard here many times in the past," continued the warrior, "and never have I gone hungry after a banquet."

"I am not hungry now," said King shortly.

"I am," said the warrior. "Just beyond that door they stack up the dishes. If you will watch here, I can go in there and eat all that I want."

"Go ahead," said the American.

"If you see an officer approaching, whistle once."

"If I see one I shall whistle. Go ahead," said King, seeing here a God-given opportunity to carry out the plan that the presence of the other warrior would have thwarted.

"It will not take me long," said the warrior, and with that

he hurried quickly toward the little door through which the slaves were carrying the food.

Scarcely had the door closed behind his companion when King crossed the apartment and leaped to the dais. At the moment the chamber was empty, not even a single slave remaining within it, and there was no witness as the American parted the hangings and disappeared through the doorway that shortly before had swallowed Lodivarman and Fou-tan.

8

❧

In the House of the King

The major-domo led Fou-tan through a dimly lighted corridor to a small apartment not far from the banquet hall. The interior walls of thin sheet lead, hand-pounded upon great blocks of stone, were covered with paintings depicting scenes of war, the chase, the palace, and the temple. There were spearmen and bowmen and great elephants trapped for war. A king upon horseback, followed by his courtiers, rode down a tiger and slew him with a spear. Countless apsarases posed in wooden postures of the dance. Priests in long robes and fantastic headdresses marched in interminable procession toward a temple to Siva, and everywhere throughout the decorations of the chamber was the symbol of the Destroyer. Upon the floor were costly rugs and the skins of tigers and leopards. There were low tables with vessels containing fruit or sweets and statuary of pottery and stone. At one side of the chamber, depending from the ceiling by three chains, swung an elaborately carved vessel from which arose the smoke and the heavy fragrance of burning incense, while upon the floor was an abundance of cushions covered by rich embroidery of many hues. The whole apartment was a blaze of colour, softened and subdued in the light of three cressets burning steadily in the quiet air.

"Why have you brought me here?" demanded Fou-tan.

"It is the will of Lodivarman, the King," replied the major-domo.

"I should be allowed three days to prepare myself," said the girl. "It is the custom."

The major-domo shook his head. "I know nothing beyond

the orders I received from Lodivarman," he said. "Customs are made by kings—and unmade."

Fou-tan looked apprehensively about her, taking in the details of the apartment. She saw that in addition to the door through which they had entered there was another door at one end of the room and that along one side there were three windows, entirely covered now by the hangings that had been drawn across them. She moved uneasily about while the major-domo remained standing, always facing her. "Will you not be seated?" he asked.

"I prefer to stand," she replied, and then, "What are your orders?"

"To bring you here," replied the major-domo.

"And that was all?"

"That was all."

"Why was I brought here?" persisted the girl.

"Because the King ordered it," replied the man.

"Why did he order it?"

"It is not for me to know or to seek to know more than the King divulges. I am but a servant." For a time the silence of the room was broken only by their breathing and the soft movements of the girl's skirt as she paced nervously the length of the gorgeous apartment that, had its walls been of cold granite, could have meant no more a prison to her.

Her thoughts were confused by the hopelessness of her situation. She had had no time to prepare for this, not in the sense of the preparation that was customary for a new bride for Lodivarman, but in a sterner, a more personal sense. She had sworn to herself that she would die before she would submit to the loathsome embraces of the Leper King; but taken thus unaware she had no means for death, so that now she concentrated every faculty of her ingenuity to discover some plan whereby she might postpone the fatal hour or find the means to liberate herself at once from the hateful crisis which she felt impended.

And then the door at the end of the room opened and Lodivarman entered. He halted just within the threshold, closing the door behind him, and stood thus for a moment in silence, his dead eyes upon her where, reacting unconsciously to a lifetime of training, she had gone on her knees before the King, as had the major-domo.

"Arise!" commanded Lodivarman, including them both in a gesture, and then he turned to the man. "You may go," he said. "See that no one enters this wing of the palace until I summon."

The major-domo, bowing low, backed from the room, closing the door softly as he departed. Then it was that Lodivarman advanced toward Fou-tan. He laid a hand upon her naked shoulder as she shrank back involuntarily.

"You fear me," he said. "To you I am a loathsome leper. They all fear me; they all hate me, but what can they do? What can you do? I am King. May the gods help the poor leper who is not a king!"

"Oh, King, I am not a king," cried the girl. "You call upon the gods to help the poor leper who is not a king, and yet you would make a leper of me, you who could save me!"

Lodivarman laughed. "Why should I spare you?" he demanded. "It was a woman who made me a leper. Let her sin be upon all women. The accursed creature! From that moment I have hated women; even while I have held them in my arms I have hated them, but some malignant demon has thwarted me. Never has a woman contracted leprosy from me; yet I always hope, and the more beautiful and young they are the higher rises my hope, for once I was young and beautiful until that accursed woman robbed me of happiness and took away from me all except the life I had grown to hate; but perhaps in you my revenge shall be consummated as I have always hoped. With you it seems that it must be fulfilled, for you are very young and by far the most beautiful woman that has been offered in atonement for the sin of her sister. I shall tell you the story; I tell it to each of them that they may know how well they deserve whatever fate the gods may hold in store for them, because, like the accursed one, they are women.

"It was many years ago. I was in the prime of my youth and my beauty. I had ridden out to hunt My Lord the Tiger with a hundred courtiers and a thousand men-at-arms. The hunt was a success. Upon that wall beside you the artist has painted Lodivarman slaying the great beast. Never shall I forget the day of our triumphal return, of Lodidhapura. Ah, Siva, no, never shall I forget. It was a day of triumph, a day of discovery, and the day of my cruel undoing by the foul creature whose sin you are to expiate.

"It was upon that day that I first tasted a mushroom. At a little village in the jungle a native upon bended knee offered me a platter of this then strange food. I partook. Never in my life had I tasted a viand more delicious. Dismounting, I sat beneath a tree before the hut of the poor peasant, and there I ate all of the mushrooms that he had prepared—a great platter of them—but I did not seem able to satisfy my craving for them, nor have I since then. I questioned him as to what they were and how they grew, and I gave orders that he be brought to Lodidhapura and given the means to propagate the royal food. He still lives. He has been showered with honours and riches, and still he raises mushrooms for Lodivarman; nor may any other in the realm raise them, nor any but the King partake of them. And thus there occurred a great happiness and a great satisfaction upon the selfsame day that saw all else snatched from me.

"As we entered Lodidhapura later in the day, crowds lined the avenue to see their King. They sang and shouted in welcome and threw blossoms at us. My charger, frightened by the noise and the bombardment of blossoms, became unmanageable, and I was hurled heavily to the ground; whereat a woman of the crowd rushed forward and threw herself upon me and with her arms about me covered my face and mouth with kisses. When my courtiers reached my side and dragged her from me and lifted me to my feet, it was seen that the woman was a leper. A great cry of horror arose, and the people who had come to applaud me shrank away, and even my courtiers drew to one side; and alone I mounted my horse and alone I rode into the city of Lodidhapura.

"Within an hour I was stricken; these hideous sores came upon my body as by magic, and never since have I been free from them. Now you shall have them, woman—daughter of a woman. As I have rotted, so shall you rot; as I am loathed, so shall you be loathed; as my youth and beauty were blasted, so shall yours be. Come!'' and he laid a heavy hand upon the arm of Fou-tan.

Gordon King, entering the dimly lighted corridor, paused a moment to listen, to note if he might not hear voices that would guide him to those he sought. As he stood there thus, he saw a door open farther along the corridor and a man back out whom he instantly recognised as the major-domo. King looked for a place to hide, but there was no hiding-place; the corridor was straight and none too wide, and it was inevitable that he would be discovered if the major-domo came that way, as he did immediately after he had closed the door of the apartment he had just quitted.

King grasped at the only chance that occurred to him for disarming the suspicions of the major-domo. Snapping to rigid attention, he stood as though a posted sentry just inside the entrance to the corridor. The major-domo saw him, and a puzzled frown crossed the man's face as he approached along the corridor, halting when he came opposite King.

''What do you here, man?'' he demanded suspiciously.

''By the command of Lodivarman, the King, I have been posted here with orders to let no one enter.''

The major-domo seemed puzzled and rather at a loss as to what action he should take in the matter. He thought of returning to Lodivarman for verification of the warrior's statement, but he knew the short temper of his King and hesitated to incur his wrath in the event that the warrior had spoken the truth. ''The King said naught to me of this,'' he said. ''He commanded me to see that no one entered this wing of the palace.''

''That is what I am here for,'' replied King; ''and, fur-thermore, I must tell you that nothing was said to me about you and, therefore, I must order you to leave at once.''

''But I am the major-domo,'' said the man haughtily.

''But I am the King's sentry,'' replied the American, ''and

if you wish to question the King's orders, let us go to Lodi-varman together and see what he has to say about it.''

''Perhaps he forgot that he had ordered a sentry posted here,'' temporised the major-domo. ''But how else could you have been posted here other than by orders from an officer of the King?''

''How else indeed?'' inquired the American.

''Very well,'' snapped the major-domo. ''See that you let no one enter,'' and he was about to pass on when King detained him.

''I have never been posted here before,'' he said; ''perhaps you had better tell me if there is any other doorway in the corridor through which anyone might enter this section of the palace, that I may watch that also; and also if there is anyone here beside the King.''

''Only the King and an apsaras are here,'' replied the man. ''They are in that room from which you saw me come. The doorway this side upon the right leads down a flight of steps to a corridor that terminates at a door opening into the royal garden at this end of the palace. It is never used except by Lodivarman, and as the door is heavily barred upon the inside and a sentry posted upon the outside, there is no likelihood that anyone will enter there, so that there remains only this doorway to be guarded.''

''My zeal shall merit the attention of the King,'' said the sentry, as the major-domo passed on into the banquet hall and disappeared from view.

The moment that the man was out of sight King hastened quickly up the corridor and paused before the door, behind which the major-domo told him he had left Lodivarman and Fou-tan. As he paused he heard a woman's voice raised in a cry of terror; it came from beyond the heavy panels of the door, and it was scarcely voiced ere Gordon King pushed the portal aside and stepped into the room.

Before him Fou-tan was struggling to release herself from the clutches of Lodivarman. Horror and revulsion were written large upon her countenance, while rage and lust distorted the hideous face of the Leper King.

At the sight of the warrior Lodivarman's face went livid with rage even greater than that which had been dominating him.

"How dare you!" he screamed. "You shall die for this. Who sent you hither?"

Gordon King closed the door behind him and advanced toward Lodivarman.

"Gordon King!" cried the girl, her astonishment reflected in her tone and in the expression upon her face. For an instant hope sprang to her eyes, but quickly it faded to be replaced by the fear that she felt for him now as well as for herself. "Oh, Gordon King, they will kill you for this!"

And now Lodivarman recognised him, too. "So you are the warrior who slew the tiger single-handed!" he cried. "What brought you here?"

"I have come for Fou-tan," said King simply.

Lodivarman's rotting face twitched with rage. He was rendered speechless by the effrontery of this low knave. Twice he tried to speak, but his anger choked him; and then he sprang for a cord that depended against one of the walls, but King guessed his purpose and forestalled him. Springing forward, he grasped Lodivarman roughly by the shoulder and hurled him back. "Not a sound out of you," he said, "or Lodidhapura will be needing a new king."

It was then that Lodivarman found his voice. "You shall be boiled in oil for this," he said in a low voice.

"Then I might as well kill you," said Gordon King, "for if I have to die, it is well that I have my vengeance first," and he raised his spear as though to cast it.

"No, no!" exclaimed Lodivarman. "Do not kill me. I grant you pardon for your great offence."

King could not but marvel at the workings of the great law of self-preservation that caused this diseased and rotten thing, burdened by misery, hatred, and unhappiness, so tenaciously to cling to the hope of life.

"Come, come!" cried Lodivarman. "Tell me what you want and be gone."

"I told you what I wanted," said King. "I came for Fou-tan."

"You cannot have her," cried Lodivarman. "She is mine. Think you that a woman would leave a king for you, knave?"

"Ask her," said King; but there was no need to ask her. Fou-tan crossed quickly to the American's side.

"Oh, Lodivarman," she cried, "let me go away in peace with this warrior."

"It is that or death, Lodivarman," said King coldly.

"That or death," repeated Lodivarman in a half whisper. "Very well, then, you have won," he added presently. "Go in peace and take the girl with you." But even if he had not noted the cunning expression in the King's eyes, Gordon King would not have been deceived by this sudden acquiescence to his demand.

"You are wise, Lodivarman," he said—"wise to choose the easiest solution to your problem. I, too, must be guided by wisdom and by my knowledge of the ways of tyrants. Lie down upon the floor."

"Why?" demanded Lodivarman. "What would you do to me? Do you forget that I am a king, that my person is holy?"

"I remember that you are a man and that men may die if, living, they present an obstacle to another man who is desperate. Lodivarman, you must know that I am desperate."

"I have told you that you might go in peace," said the monarch. "Why would you humiliate me?"

"I have no desire to humiliate you, Lodivarman. I only wish to assure myself that you will not be able to give the alarm before Fou-tan and I are beyond the walls of Lodi-dhapura. I would secure you so that you cannot leave this chamber; and as you have given orders that no one is to enter this part of the King's house until you summon, it will be morning, at least, before you can despatch warriors in pursuit of us."

"He speaks the truth," said Fou-tan to the King; "you will not be harmed."

For a moment Lodivarman stood silent as though in thought, and then suddenly and quite unexpectedly he leaped straight for King, striking up the warrior's spear and endeavouring to clutch him by the throat. Lodivarman was no coward.

So impetuous was the leper's charge that King was borne backward beneath the man's weight. His heel caught in the fold of a tiger skin upon the floor, and he fell heavily backward with Lodivarman upon him. The fingers of the leper were already at his throat; the rotting face was close to his; the odour of fetid breath was in his nostrils. But only for an instant did the Khmer King have an advantage. As he raised his voice to summon help, the hand of the American found his throat, choking out the sound even as it was born. Youth and strength and endurance all were upon the side of the younger man. Slowly he wormed his body from beneath that of the King; and then, kicking one of Lodivarman's braced feet from beneath him, he rolled the Khmer over upon his back and was upon him. Lodivarman's grip was wrenched from King's throat, and now the Khmer was gasping for breath as he fought, violently but futilely, to disengage himself from the clutches of the man upon him.

"Lie still," said King. "Do not force me to kill you." The repulsive sores upon the face of the King were directly beneath his eyes. Even in this tense moment that was so closely approaching tragedy, the habits of his medical training were still sufficiently strong to cause the American to give considerably more than cursory attention to these outward physical symptoms of the dread disease that had given Lodivarman the name of the Leper King; and what the doctor in him saw induced a keen regret that he could not investigate this strange case more fully.

At King's last command and threat, Lodivarman had ceased his struggles, and the American had relaxed his grasp upon the other's throat. "Are there any cords attached to the hangings in the room, Fou-tan?" he demanded of the girl.

"Yes, there are cords at the windows," replied she.

"Get them for me," said the American.

Quickly Fou-tan wrenched the cords loose from their fastenings and brought them to King, and with them the man bound the wrists and ankles of the Khmer King. So securely did he bind them and so tightly did he tie the knots that he had no fear that Lodivarman could release himself without aid; and now to be doubly certain that he could not summon assistance, King stuffed a gag of soft cloth into the mouth of his royal prisoner and bound it tightly there with another cord. Then he sprang to his feet.

"Come, Fou-tan," he said, "we have no time to lose; but wait, you cannot go abroad in that garb. You are to accompany me as a slave girl, not as an apsaras."

Fou-tan snatched off her ornate headdress and threw it upon the floor; then she loosened the golden girdle that held her voluminous skirt in place, and as it dropped to the floor King saw that she wore a silken sampot beneath it. Across a taboret was a long drape, the ends of which were spread upon the floor. This Fou-tan took and wound about her lithe form as a sarong.

"I am ready, Gordon King," she said.

"The ear-rings," he suggested, "the necklace, and your other wrist ornaments. They look too royal for a slave."

"You are right," she said, as she removed them.

King quickly extinguished the cressets, leaving the room in darkness. Then together the two groped their way to the door. Opening it a little, King looked about. The corridor was empty. He drew Fou-tan into it and closed the door behind him. To the next door in the corridor he stepped and tried it; it was not locked. He could just see the top of a flight of stone steps leading down into utter darkness. He wished that he had brought one of the cressets, but now it was too late. He drew Fou-tan within and closed the door, and now they could see nothing.

"Where does this lead?" asked Fou-tan in a whisper.

"It is the King's private passage to the garden," replied the American, "and if I have made no mistake in my calculations, the other end of it is guarded by a sentry who will pass us with a wink."

As they groped their way slowly down the steps and along the corridor King explained to Fou-tan the subterfuge he had adopted to obtain a place upon the guard that night and that he had particularly noticed the little door at the end of this wing of the palace and when the major-domo had told him of the private passage leading to the garden he had guessed that it ended at this very door. "The sentry there," he had concluded, "is from my own barracks and knows the story. That is why you must be a little slave girl to-night, Fou-tan."

"I do not mind being a slave girl—now," she said, and King felt the little fingers of the hand he held press his own more tightly.

They came at last to the end of the corridor. In the darkness King's fingers ran over the surface of the door in search of bars and bolts. The fastening, which he found at last, was massive but simple. It moved beneath the pressure of his hand with only a slight grating sound. He pushed the door slowly open; the fresh night air blew in upon them; the starlit heavens bathed the garden in gentle luminosity. Cautiously King crossed the threshold. He saw the warrior upon his post without, and instantly the man saw him.

"Who comes?" demanded the sentry, dropping his spear-point on a level with King's breast as he wheeled quickly toward him.

"It is I—King—of Vama's ten. I have found the slave girl of whom I told you, and I would walk in the garden with her for a few moments."

"I do not know you," snapped the warrior. "I never heard of you or your slave girl," and then it was that King realised that he had never seen this man before—that the sentries had been changed since he had entered the palace. His heart sank within him, yet he maintained a bold front.

"It will do no harm to let us pass for a while," he said, "you can see that I am a member of the guard, as otherwise I could not have gained access to the King's house."

"That may be true," replied the warrior, "but I have my orders that no one shall pass either in or out of this doorway without proper authority. I will summon an officer. If he wishes to let you pass, that is none of my affair."

Fou-tan had been standing at King's side. Now she moved

slowly and languorously toward the sentry. Every undulating motion of her lithe body was provocative. She came very close to him and turned her beautiful face up toward his. Her eyes were dreamy wells of promise. "For me?" she asked in a soft, caressing voice. "For me, warrior, could you not be blind for a moment?"

"For you, yes," said the man huskily, "but you are not for me; you belong to him."

"I have a sister," suggested Fou-tan. "When I return within the King's house, perhaps she will come to this little door. What do you say, warrior?"

"Perhaps it can do no harm," he said hesitatingly. "How long will you remain in the garden?"

"We shall be in the garden only a few minutes," said King.

"I shall turn my back," said the sentry. "I have not seen you. Remember that, I have not seen you."

"Nor have we seen you," replied King.

"Do not forget your sister, little one," said the sentry, as he turned away from them and continued along his post, while Gordon King and Fou-tan merged with the shadows of the trees beyond.

Perhaps, hours later, when he was relieved, the sentry realised that he had been duped, but there were excellent reasons why he should keep a still tongue in his head, though he intended at first opportunity to look up this warrior who said that his name was King and demand an accounting from him. Perhaps, after all, the slave girl had had no sister, with which thought he turned on his pallet of straw and fell asleep.

9

The Flight

True to their promise to the sentry, Fou-tan and King did not remain long within the garden of Lodivarman, the Leper King. Inasmuch as the walls had been built to keep people out of the royal enclosure, rather than to keep them in, it was not difficult to find a spot where they might be scaled, since in many places trees grew near, their branches overhanging.

Along the unlighted streets of the city proper the sight of a warrior and a girl was not so uncommon as to attract attention, and so it was with comparative ease that they made their way to the city's outer wall. Here, once more, a like condition prevailed. Low sheds and buildings abutted against the inner surface of the city's ramparts, and presently King found a place where they could ascend to the roof of a building and surmount the wall itself. The drop to the ground upon the outside, however, was considerable, and here they were confronted with the greatest danger that had menaced them since they had passed the sentry. For either one of them to suffer a sprained ankle or a broken leg at this time would have been fatal to both.

In the darkness King could not determine the nature of the ground at the foot of the wall; the light of the stars was not sufficient for that.

"We shall have to take a chance here, Fou-tan," he said.

"It is high, Gordon King; but if you tell me to I will jump."

"No," he said, "that is not necessary. I judge that the wall is about twenty feet high here. My spear is six feet long; your sarong must be at least eight feet, possibly longer."

96

"Yes, it is much too long," she said; "it was not intended for a sarong. But what has that to do with it?"

"I am going to tie one end of the sarong to the end of my spear; I shall tie a knot in the other end of the sarong. Do you think that you are strong enough to cling to that knot while I lower you as near the ground as I can?"

"I am very strong," said Fou-tan, "and desperation lends even greater strength." As she spoke she commenced to remove her sarong, and a moment later King was lowering her slowly over the edge of the wall.

"When I have lowered you as far as I can," he whispered in her ear, "I shall tell you to drop. After you have done so, stand quickly to one side, and I will drop my spear. Then you must take it away so that I will not fall upon it; and also if the ground is rough, smooth it a little for me."

"Yes," she said, and King lowered her away down the outside of the wall of Lodidhapura.

Presently he was clinging only to the end of the spear and was leaning far over the edge of the wall. "Drop," he said in a low voice. Instantly the pull of her weight was gone from the spear handle in his hand. "Are you all right?" he asked in a low voice.

"Yes," she replied. "Drop the spear," and then an instant later: "the grass is thick and soft here."

King lowered himself over the edge of the wall and hung an instant by his fingers. Then he released his hold and dropped. As he rolled over in the tall grass, considerably jarred but unhurt, Fou-tan was at his side. "You are all right, Gordon King?" she demanded. "You are not hurt?"

"I am all right," he said.

"I shall sacrifice a bullock in the temple of Siva when we reach Pnom Dhek," she said.

"For your sake, Fou-tan, I hope that it will not be long before you are able to sacrifice the bullock, but we are not at Pnom Dhek yet; I do not even know where it is."

"I do," replied the girl.

"In what direction?" he asked.

She pointed. "There," she said, "but the way is long and difficult."

Near them was a group of native huts, clustered close to the foot of the wall, and so they moved out straight across the clearing to the edge of the jungle and then, turning, paralleled the jungle until they had passed the city.

"When we were brought into Lodidhapura I saw an avenue leading into the jungle somewhere in this direction," said King.

"Yes," replied Fou-tan, "but that does not lead to Pnom Dhek."

"Which is the reason that I wish to find it," said King. "The pursuit will be directed straight in the direction of Pnom Dhek, you may be assured. Men upon elephants and upon horses will travel after us much more rapidly than we can travel and we shall be overtaken if we take the road toward Pnom Dhek. We must go in some other direction and hide in the jungle for days, perhaps, before we may dare to approach Pnom Dhek."

"I do not care," she said, "and I shall not be afraid if you are with me, Gordon King."

It was not long before they found the road that he sought. In the open starlit night the transition to the jungle was depressing and, too, as they both realised, it was highly dangerous. All about them were the noises of the gloomy nocturnal forest: the mysterious rustling of underbrush as some beast passed on padded feet, a coughing growl in the distance, a snarl and a scream, followed by a long silence that was more terrifying than the noise.

A few months ago King would have considered their position far more precarious than he did this night, but now long familiarity with the jungle had so inured him to its dangers that he had unwittingly acquired that tendency to fatalism that is a noticeable characteristic of primitive people who live constantly beneath the menace of beasts of prey. He was, however, no less aware of the dangers that confronted them, but held them the lesser of two evils. To remain in the neighbourhood of Lodidhapura would most certainly result in their early capture and subject them to a fate more merciless and more cruel than any which might waylay them along the dark aisles of the forest. Propinquity had considerably altered his estimation of the great cats; whereas formerly he had thought of them as the fearless exterminators of mankind; he had since learned that not all of them are mankillers and that more often did they avoid man than pursue him. The chances, then, that they might come through the night without attack were greatly in their favour; but should they meet a tiger or a leopard or a panther which, because of hunger, old age, or viciousness, should elect to attack them, their doom might well be sealed; and whether they were moving away from Lodidhapura upon the ground or hiding in a tree, they would be almost equally at the mercy of one or another of these fierce carnivores.

The avenue that they were following, which entered the jungle from Lodidhapura, ran broad and clear for a considerable distance into the forest, dwindling at last to little more than an ordinary game-trail. To elude their pursuers, they must leave it; but that they might not attempt until daylight, since to strike out blindly into the trackless jungle, buried in the impenetrable gloom of night, must almost assuredly have spelled disaster.

"Even if they find Lodivarman before morning," he said, "I doubt that they will commence their search for us before daylight."

"They will be ordered out in pursuit the instant that Lodivarman can issue a command," replied Fou-tan; "but there is little likelihood that anyone will dare to risk his anger by approaching the apartment in which he lies until his long silence has aroused suspicion. If your bonds hold and he is unable to remove the gag from his mouth, I doubt very much that he will be discovered before noon. His people fear his anger, which is quick and merciless, and there is only one man in all Lodidhapura who would risk incurring it by entering that apartment before Lodivarman summoned him."

"And who is that?" asked King.

"Vay Thon, the high priest of Siva," replied the girl.

"If I am missed and the word reaches the ears of Vay Thon," said King, "it is likely that his suspicion may be aroused."

"Why?" asked Fou-tan.

"Because I talked with him this afternoon, and I could see that he guessed what was in my heart. It was he who told me that Lodivarman would send for you to-night. It was Vay Thon who warned me to attempt no rash deed."

"He does not love Lodivarman," said the girl, "and it may be that if he guessed the truth he might be silent, for he has been kind to me; and I know that he liked you."

For hour after hour the two groped their way along the dark trail, aided now by the dim light of the moon that the canopy of foliage above blocked and diffused until that which reached the jungle floor could not be called light at all, but rather a lesser degree of darkness.

With the passing of the hours King realised that Fou-tan's steps were commencing to lag. He timed his own then to suit hers and, walking close beside her, supported her with his arm. She seemed so small and delicate and unsuited to an ordeal like this that the man marvelled at her stamina. More of a hot-house plant than a girl of flesh and blood seemed Fou-tan of Pnom Dhek, and yet she was evincing the courage and endurance of a man. He recalled that not once during the night had she voiced any fear of the jungle, not even when great beasts had passed so close to them that they could almost hear their breathing. If Khmer slaves were of this stock, to what noble heights of courage must the masters achieve!

"You are very tired, Fou-tan," he said; "we shall rest presently."

"No," she replied. "Do not stop on my account. If you would not rest upon your own account, it must be that you do not think it wise to do so; that I am with you should make no difference. When you feel the need of rest and believe that it is safe to rest, then I may rest also, but not until then."

Stealthily the dawn, advance guard of the laggard day, crept slowly through the jungle, pushing back the impenetrable shadows of the night. Shadowy trees emerged from the darkness; armies of gaunt grey boles marched in endless procession slowly by them; the trail that had been but a blank wall of darkness before projected itself forward to the next turn; the hideous night lay behind them, and a new hope was born within their bosoms. It was time now to leave the trail and search for a hiding-place, and conditions were particularly favourable at this spot, since the underbrush was comparatively scant.

Turning abruptly to the left, King struck off at right angles to the trail; and for another hour the two pushed onward into the untracked mazes of the forest. This last hour was particularly difficult, for there was no trail and the ground rose rapidly, suggesting to King that they were approaching mountains. There were numerous outcroppings of rocks; and at length they came to the edge of a gorge, in the bottom of which ran a stream of pure water.

"The gods have been good to us," exclaimed King.

"I have been praying to them all night," said Fou-tan.

The little stream had cut deeply into its limestone bed; but at last they found a way down to the water, where the cool and refreshing liquid gave them renewed strength and hope.

The evidences of erosion in the limestone about them suggested to King that a little search might reveal a safe and adequate hiding-place. Fortunately the water in the stream was low, giving them dry footing along its side as they followed the gorge upward; nor had they gone far before they discovered a location that was ideal for their purpose. Here the stream made a sharp bend that was almost a right angle; and where the waters had rushed for countless ages against the base of a limestone cliff, they had eaten their way far into it, hollowing out a sanctuary where the two fugitives would be safe from observation from above.

Leaving Fou-tan in the little grotto, King crossed the stream and gathered an armful of dry grasses that grew above the high water-line upon the opposite side. After several trips he was able to make a reasonably comfortable bed for each of them.

"Sleep now," he said to Fou-tan; "and when you are rested, I shall sleep."

The girl would have demurred, wishing him to sleep first; but even as she voiced her protest, exhaustion overcame her and she sank into a profound slumber. Seated with his back against the limestone wall of their retreat, King sought desperately to keep awake; but the monotonous sound of the running water, which drowned all other sounds, acted as a soporific, which, combined with outraged Nature's craving for rest, made the battle he was waging a difficult one. Twice he dozed and then, disgusted with himself, he arose and paced to and fro the length of their sanctuary, but the instant that he sat down again he was gone.

It was mid-afternoon when King awoke with a start. He had been the victim of a harrowing dream, so real that even as he awoke he grasped his spear and leaped to his feet, but there was no danger menacing. He listened intently, but the only sound came from the leaping waters of the stream.

Fou-tan opened her eyes and looked at him. "What is it?" she asked.

He grimaced in self-disgust. "I slept at my post," he said. "I have been asleep a long time, and I have just awakened."

"I am glad," she said with a smile. "I hope that you have slept for a long time."

"I have slept almost as long as you have, Fou-tan," he replied; "but suppose that they had come while I slept."

"They did not come, however," she reminded him.

"Well, right or wrong, we have both slept now," he said, "and my next business is to obtain food."

"There is plenty in the forest," she said.

"Yes, I noted it as we came this way in the morning."

"Will it be safe to go out and search for food?" asked the girl.

"We shall have to take the chance," he replied. "We must eat and we cannot find food at night. We shall have to go together, Fou-tan, as I cannot risk leaving you alone for a moment."

As King and Fou-tan left their hiding-place and started

down the gorge toward a place where they could clamber out of it into the forest in search of food, a creature at the summit of the cliff upon the opposite side of the stream crouched behind a low bush and watched them. Out of small eyes, deep-set beneath a mass of tangled hair, the creature watched every movement of the two; and when they had passed, it followed them stealthily, stalking them as a tiger might have stalked. But this was no tiger; it was a man—a huge, hulking brute of a man, standing well over six-feet-six on its great flat feet. Its only apparel was a G string, made from the skin of a wild animal. It wore no ornaments, but it carried weapons—a short spear, a bow, and arrows.

The jungle lore that the American had learned under the tutorage of Che stood him in good stead now, for it permitted him quickly to locate edible fruit and tubers without waste of time and with a minimum of effort. Fou-tan, city-bred, had but a hazy and most impractical knowledge of the flora of the jungle. She knew the tall, straight teak standing leafless now in the dry season and the India-rubber tree; and with almost childish delight she recognised the leathery laurel-like leaves of the tree from whose gum resin gamboge is secured; the tall, flowering stems of the cardamon she knew too; but the sum total of her knowledge would not have given sustenance to a canary in the jungle. It was therefore that King's efficiency in this matter filled her with awe and admiration. Her dark eyes followed his every move; and when he had collected all of the food that they could conveniently carry and they had turned their steps back toward their hiding-place, Fou-tan was bubbling over with pride and confidence and happiness. Perhaps it was as well that she did not see the uncouth figure hiding in the underbrush as they passed.

Back in their retreat they partially satisfied their hunger with such of the food as did not require cooking. "To-night we can have a fire," said King, "and roast some of these tubers. It would not be safe now, for the smoke might be seen for a considerable distance; but at night they will not be searching for us, and the light of a small fire will never escape from this gorge."

After they had eaten, King took his spear and walked down to the stream where he had seen fish jumping. He was prompted more by a desire to pass away the time than by any hope of success in this piscatorial adventure, but so numerous were the fish and so unafraid that he succeeded in spearing two with the utmost ease while Fou-tan stood at his elbow applauding him with excited little exclamations and squeals of delight.

King had never been any less sensitive to the approbation of the opposite sex than any other normal man, but never, he realised, had praise sounded more sweetly in his ears than now. There was something so altogether sincere in Fou-tan's praise that it never even remotely suggested adulation. He had always found her such an altogether forthright little person that he could never doubt her sincerity.

"Now we shall have a feast," she exclaimed, as they carried the fishes back into their grotto. "It is a good thing for me that you are here, Gordon King, and not another."

"Why, Fou-tan?" he asked.

"Imagine Bharata Rahon or any of the others being faced with the necessity of finding food for me here in the jungle!" she exclaimed. "Why, I should either have starved to death or have been poisoned by their ignorance and stupidity. No, there is no one like Gordon King, as Fou-tan, his slave, should know."

"Do not call yourself that," he said. "You are not my slave."

"Let us play that I am," she said. "I like it. A slave is great in the greatness of his master; therefore, it can be no disgrace to be the slave of Gordon King."

"If I had not found you here in the jungles of Cambodia," he said; "I could have sworn that you are Irish."

"Irish?" she asked. "What is Irish?"

"The Irish are a people who live upon a little island far, far away. They have a famous stone there, and when one has kissed this stone he cannot help thereafter speaking in terms of extravagant praise of all whom he meets. It is said that all of the Irish have kissed this stone."

"I do not have to kiss a stone to tell the truth to you, Gordon King," she said. "I do not always say nice things to people, but I like to say them to you."

"Why?" he asked.

"I do not know, Gordon King," said Fou-tan, and her eyes dropped from his level gaze.

They were sitting upon the dry grasses that he had gathered for their beds. King sat now in silence, looking at the girl. For the thousandth time he was impressed by her great beauty, and then the face of another girl arose in a vision between them. It was the face of Susan Anne Prentice. With a short laugh King turned his gaze down toward the stream; while once again, upon the opposite cliff-top, the little eyes of the great man watched them.

"Why do you laugh, Gordon King?" asked Fou-tan, looking up suddenly.

"You would not understand, Fou-tan," he said. He had been thinking of what Susan Anne would say could she have knowledge of the situation in which he then was—a situation which he realised was not only improbable but impossible. Here was he, Gordon King, a graduate physician, a perfectly normal product of the twentieth century, sitting almost naked under a big rock with a little slave girl of a race that had disappeared hundreds of years before. That in itself was preposterous. But there was another matter that was even less credible; he realised that he enjoyed the situation, and most of all he enjoyed the company of the little slave girl.

"You are laughing at me, Gordon King," said Fou-tan, "and I do not like to be laughed at."

"I was not laughing at you, Fou-tan," he replied. "I could not laugh at you. I—"

"You what?" she demanded.

"I could not laugh at you," he replied lamely.

"You said that once before, Gordon King," she reminded him. "You started to say something else. What was it?"

For a moment he was silent. "I have forgotten, Fou-tan," he said then.

His eyes were turned away from her as she looked at him

keenly in silence for some time. Then a slow smile lighted her face and she broke into a little humming song.

The man upon the opposite cliff withdrew stealthily until he was out of sight of the two in the gorge below him. Then he arose to an erect position and crept softly away into the forest. Ready in his hands were his bow and an arrow. For all his great size and weight he moved without noise, his little eyes shifting constantly from side to side. Suddenly, and so quickly that one could scarcely follow the movements of his hands, an arrow sped from his bow, and an instant later he stepped forward and picked up a large rat that had been transfixed by his missile. The creature moved slowly onward, and presently a little monkey swung through the trees above him. Again the bowstring twanged, and the little monkey hurtled to the ground at the feet of the primitive hunter. Squatting on his haunches the man-thing ate the rat raw; then he carried the monkey back to the edge of the gorge, and after satisfying himself that the two were still there he fell to upon the principal item of his dinner; and he was still eating when darkness came.

Fou-tan had not broken King's embarrassed silence, but presently the man arose. "Where are you going, Gordon King?" she asked.

"There is some driftwood lodged upon the opposite bank, left there by last season's flood waters. We shall need it for our cooking fire to-night."

"I will go with you and help you," said Fou-tan, and together they crossed the little stream and gathered the dry wood for their fire.

From Che and Kangrey the American had learned to make fire without matches; and he soon had a little blaze burning, far back beneath the shelter of their overhanging rock. He had cleaned and washed the fish and now proceeded to grill them over the fire, while Fou-tan roasted two large tubers impaled upon the ends of sticks.

"I would not exchange this for the palace of a king, Gordon King," she said.

"Nor I, Fou-tan," he replied.

"Are you happy, Gordon King?" she asked.

"Yes," he replied. "And you, Fou-tan, are you happy?"

She nodded her head. "It is because you and I are together," she said simply.

"We come from opposite ends of the earth, Fou-tan," he said, "we are separated by centuries of time, we have nothing in common, your world and my world are as remote from one another as the stars; and yet, Fou-tan, it seems as though I had known you always. It does not seem possible that I have lived all my life up to now without even knowing that you existed."

"I have felt that too, Gordon King," said the girl. "I cannot understand it, but it is so. However, you are wrong in one respect."

"And what is that?" he asked.

"You said that we had nothing in common. We have."

"What is it?" demanded King.

Fou-tan shuddered. "The leprosy," she said. "He touched us both. We shall both have it."

Gordon King laughed. "We shall never contract leprosy from Lodivarman," he said. "I am a doctor. I know."

"Why shall we not?" she demanded.

"Because Lodivarman is not a leper," replied the American.

10

Love and the Brute

From the opposite side of the gorge the brute, gnawing upon a leg bone of the monkey, watched the two below. He saw the fire kindled and it troubled him. He was afraid of fire. Muddily, in his undeveloped brain, it represented the personification of some malign power. The brute knew no god; but he knew that there were forces that brought pain, disaster, death, and that oftentimes these forces were invisible. The visible causes of such effects were the enemies he had met in the jungle in the form of men or of beasts; therefore, it was natural that he should endow the invisible causes of similar effects with the physical attributes of the enemies that he could see. He peopled the jungle accordingly with invisible men and invisible beasts that wrought pain, disaster, and death. These enemies he held in far greater fear than those that were visible to him. Fire, he knew, was the work of one of these dread creatures, and the very sight of it made him uncomfortable.

The brute was not hungry; he harboured no animosity for the two creatures he stalked; he was motivated by a more powerful urge than hunger or hate. He had seen the girl!

The fire annoyed him and kept him at bay; but time meant little to the brute. He saw that the two had made beds, and he guessed that they would sleep where they were during the night. On the morrow they would go out after food, and there would be no fire with them. The brute was content to wait until the morrow. He found some tall grass and, getting upon his hands and knees, turned about several times, as bedding dogs are wont to do, and then lay down. He had flattened the grasses so that they all lay in one direction, and when he turned upon his bed he always turned in that direction, so that the sharp ends of the grasses did not stick into his flesh. Perhaps he had learned this trick from the wild dogs, or perhaps the wild dogs first learned it from man. Who knows?

In the darkness Fou-tan and King sat upon their beds and talked. Fou-tan was full of questions. She wanted to know all about the strange country from which King came. Most of the things he told her she could not understand; but her questions were quite often directed upon subjects that were well within her ken—there are some matters that are eternal; time does not alter them.

"Are the women of your country beautiful?" she asked.

"Some of them," replied the man.

"Have you a wife, Gordon King?" The question was voiced in a whisper.

"No, Fou-tan."

"But you love someone," she insisted, for love is so important to a woman that she cannot imagine a life devoid of love.

"I have been too busy to fall in love," he replied good-naturedly.

"You are not very busy now," suggested Fou-tan.

"I think I shall be a very busy man for the next few days trying to get you back to Pnom Dhek," he assured her.

Fou-tan was silent. It was so dark that he could scarcely see her. But he could feel her presence near him, and it seemed to exert as strong an influence upon him as might have physical contact. He had recognised the power of that indefinable thing called personality when he had talked with people and looked into their eyes; but he never had had it reach out through the dark and lay hold of him as though with warm fingers of flesh and blood, and King found the sensation most disquieting.

They lay in silence upon their beds of dry grasses, each occupied with his own thoughts. The heat of the jungle day was rising slowly from the narrow gorge, and a damp chill was replacing it. The absolute darkness which surrounded them was slightly mitigated in their immediate vicinity by an occasional flame rising from the embers of their dying fire as some drying twigs of their fuel ignited. King was thinking of the girl at his side, of the responsibility which her presence entailed, and of the duty that he owed to her and to himself. He tried not to think about her, but that he found impossible, and the more that she was in his mind the stronger became the realisation of the hold that she had obtained upon him; that the sensation that she animated within him was love seemed incredibly preposterous. He tried to assure himself that it was but an infatuation engendered by her beauty and propinquity, and he girded himself to conquer his infatuation that he might perform the duty that had devolved upon him in so impersonal a way that there might be no regret.

In order to fortify this noble decision he cast Fou-tan from his mind entirely and occupied himself with thoughts of his friends in far-away America. In retrospect he laughed and danced again with Susan Anne Prentice; he listened to her pleasant cultured voice and enjoyed once more the sweet companionship of the girl who was to him all that a beloved sister might have been; and then a little sigh came from the bed of grasses at his side, and the vision of Susan Anne Prentice faded into oblivion.

Again there was a long silence, broken only by the murmur of the tumbling stream.

"Gordon King!" It was just a whisper.

"What is it, Fou-tan?"

"I am afraid, Gordon King," said the girl. How like a little child in the dark she sounded. Before he could answer, there came the sound of a soft thud down the gorge and the rattle of loose earth falling from above.

"What was that?" asked Fou-tan in a frightened whisper. "Something is coming, Gordon King. Look!"

Silently the man rose to his feet, grasping his spear in readiness. Down the gorge he saw two blazing points of flame; and quickly stepping to their fire, he placed dry twigs upon the embers, blowing upon them gently until they burst into flame. At a little distance those two glowing spots burned out of the darkness.

King piled more wood upon the fire until it blazed up bravely, illuminating their little grotto and revealing Fou-tan sitting up upon her bed of grasses, gazing with wide horror-filled eyes at those two silent, ominous harbingers of death fixed so menacingly upon them. "My Lord the Tiger!" she whispered; and her low, tense tones were vibrant with all the inherent horror of the great beast that had been passed down to her by countless progenitors, for whom My Lord the Tiger had constituted life's greatest menace.

Primitive creatures, constantly surrounded by lethal dangers, sleep lightly. The descent of the great cat into the gorge, followed by the sounds of the falling earth and stones it had dislodged, brought to his feet the sleeping brute upon the opposite summit. Thinking that the noise might have come from the quarry in the gorge below, the creature moved quickly to the edge of the cliff and looked down; and as the mounting blazes of King's fire illuminated the scene, the brute saw the great tiger standing with upraised head, watching the man and the woman in their rocky retreat.

Here was an interloper that aroused the ire of the brute; here was a deadly enemy about to seize that which the brute had already marked as his own. The creature selected a heavy arrow, the heaviest arrow that he carried, and, fitting it to his bow, he bent the sturdy weapon until the point of the arrow touched the fingers of his bow-hand; then he let drive at a point just behind the shoulders of the tiger.

What happened thereafter happened very quickly. The arrow drove through to the great cat's lungs; the shock, the surprise and the pain brought instant reaction. Not having sensed the presence of any other formidable creature than those before him, My Lord the Tiger must naturally have assumed that they were the authors of his hurt. This supposition, at least, seemed likely if judged by that which immediately occurred.

With a hideous roar, with blazing eyes, with wide distended jaws, revealing gleaming fangs, the great cat charged straight for King. Into the circle of firelight it bounded like a personification of some hideous force of destruction.

Little Fou-tan, on her feet beside King, seized a blazing brand from the fire and hurled it full into the face of the charging beast; but the tiger was too far gone in pain and rage longer to harbour fear of aught.

King's spear-arm went back. Through his mind flashed the recollection of the other tiger that he had killed with a single spear cast. He had known then that he had been for the instant the favoured child of Fortune. The laws of chance would never countenance a repetition of that amazing stroke of luck; yet there was naught that he could do but try.

He held his nerves and muscles in absolute control, the servants of his iron will. Every faculty of mind and body was centred upon the accuracy and the power of his spear-arm. Had he given thought to what might follow, his nerves must necessarily have faltered, but he did not. Cool and collected, he waited until he knew that he could not miss nor wait another moment. Then the bronze skin of his spear-arm flashed in the light of the fire, and at the same instant he swept Fou-tan to him with his left arm and leaped to one side.

Not even My Lord the Tiger could have acted with greater celerity, calmness, and judgment. A low grunt of surprise and admiration burst from the lips of the brute watching from the summit of the opposite cliff.

The charge of the tiger carried it full into the fire, scattering the burning branches in all directions. The dry grasses of the beds burst into flame. Blinded and terrified, the tiger looked about futilely for his prey; but King had leaped quickly across the stream to the opposite side of the gorge, having learned by experience that a creature near the fire can see nothing in the outer darkness. The great cat, clawing and biting at the spear protruding from its chest, rent the air with its screams of pain and growls of rage. Suddenly it was quiet, standing like a yellow and black statue carved from gold and ebony; then it took a few steps forward, sagged, and slumped lifeless to the ground.

Gordon King felt very weak in the knees, so weak that he sat down quite suddenly. He had rung the bell twice in succession, but he could scarcely believe the evidence of his own eyes. Fou-tan came and sat down close beside him and rested her cheek against his arm. "My Gordon King!" she murmured softly.

Almost without volition he put his arm about her. "My Fou-tan!" he said. The girl snuggled close in his embrace.

For a time they sat watching the tiger, hesitating to approach lest there might remain a spark of life within the great form, each knowing that one little instant of life would be sufficient to destroy them both were they near the beast; but the great cat never moved again.

The dissipated fire was dying down, and realising more than ever now the necessity for keeping it up, King and Fou-tan arose and, crossing the stream, scraped together the remaining embers of their fire and rebuilt it with fresh wood.

From the cliff above the brute watched them, and once again grunted his admiration as he saw King withdraw his spear from the body of the fallen tiger. Placing one foot against the breast of the great beast, the American was forced to exert every ounce of his weight and strength to withdraw the weapon, so deeply was it embedded in the bone and sinew of its victim.

"I am afraid that we shall not get much sleep tonight, Fou-tan," said King as he returned to the fire.

"I am not sleepy," replied the girl; "I could not sleep, and then, too, it is commencing to get cold. I would rather sit here by the fire until morning. I would rather have my eyes open than closed in the night when My Lord the Tiger walks abroad."

Once more they sat down side by side, their backs against the rocky wall that had been warmed by the heat of the nearby fire.

The brute, realising that they had settled themselves for the night, returned to his primitive bed and settled himself once more for sleep.

Fou-tan cuddled close to Gordon King; his arm was about

her. He felt her soft hair against his cheek. He drew her closer to him. "Fou-tan!" he said.

"Yes, Gordon King, what is it?" she asked. He noted that her voice trembled.

"I love you," said Gordon King.

A sigh that came in little gasps was his reply. He felt her heart pounding against his side.

A soft arm crept upward to encircle his neck, drawing him gently down to the sweet face turned toward his. Eyes, dimmed with unshed tears, gazed into his eyes. Trembling lips fluttered beneath his lips, and then he crushed her to him in the first kiss of love.

The flower-like beauty of the girl, her softness, her help-lessness, combined with the exaltation of this, his first love, enveloped Fou-tan with an aura of sanctity that rendered her almost an object of veneration in the eyes of the man—a high priestess enshrined in the Holy of Holies of his heart. He marvelled that he had won the love of so glorious a creature. The little slave girl became an angel, and he her paladin. In this thought lay the secret of King's attitude toward Fou-tan. He was glad that she was small and helpless, for he liked to think of himself as her champion and protector. He liked to feel that the safety of the girl he loved lay in his hands and that he was physically and morally competent to discharge the obligations that Fate had reposed within him.

Despite the fact that she was soft and small, Fou-tan was not without self-reliance and courage, as she had amply proved when she had run away from the palace of Lodivar-man and risked the perils of the savage jungle; yet she was still so wholly feminine that she found her greatest happiness in the protection of the man she loved.

"I am very happy," whispered Fou-tan.

"And so am I," said King, "happier than I have ever been before in my life, but now we must make our plans all anew."

"What do you mean?" she asked.

"We may not go to Pnom Dhek now. We must find our way out of the jungle so that I can take you to my own country."

"Why?" she demanded.

"Before I answer you," he replied, "there is one question that I have not asked but that you must answer before we make our plans for the future."

"What is that?" she asked.

"Will you be my wife, Fou-tan?"

"Oh, Gordon King, I have answered that already, for I have told you that I love you. Fou-tan would not tell any man that whom she could not or would not take as her husband; but what has that to do with our returning to Pnom Dhek?"

"It was everything to do with it," replied King, "because I will not take the woman who is to be my wife back into slavery."

She looked up into his face, her eyes alight with a new happiness and understanding. "Now I may never doubt that you love me, Gordon King," she said.

He looked at her questioningly. "I do not understand what you mean," he said.

"Though you thought that I was born a slave, you asked me to be your wife," she said.

"You told me from the first that you were a slave girl," he reminded her.

"I was a slave girl in Lodidhapura," she explained, "but in Pnom Dhek I am no slave. I must return there to my father's house. It is my duty. When the King learns what a great warrior you are, he will give you a place in his guard. Then you will be able to take a wife, and, perhaps, my father will not object."

"And if he does?" asked King.

"Let us not think of that," replied Fou-tan.

As the night wore on, a slow rain commenced to fall, herald of the coming rainy season. King kept the fire replenished, and its heat warmed them as they sat and talked of their future, or spoke in half-awed whispers of the transcendent happiness that had come into their lives.

Before dawn the rain ceased and the skies cleared, and when the sun rose he looked upon a steaming jungle, where strange odours, long imprisoned by drought, filled the air as they wandered through the forest.

King rose and stretched himself. Near him the carcass of the great beast he had slain aroused within him regret that he must leave such a trophy to the carrion creatures or to decay.

From the tiger's back protruded the feathered shaft of an arrow. King was puzzled. He tugged upon the missile and withdrew it. It was a crude thing—much more primitive than those made by Che. It created a mystery that appeared little likely of solution. The best that he could do was guess that the tiger had carried it for some time before he attacked them. Then, for the time, he forgot the matter, which later was to be recalled in poignant grief.

Across the gorge the brute bestirred himself. He had lain quietly throughout the rain, keeping the spot beneath him dry. Physical discomfort meant little to him; he was accustomed to it. He arose, and, like King, stretched himself. Then he crept to the edge of the gorge and looked down at the man and the woman.

Fou-tan, who had been dozing, awoke now and rose to her feet. With the undulating grace of youth and health and physical perfection she came and stood beside King. She leaned close against the man, who put an arm about her and, bending, kissed her upturned mouth. The brute moistened his thick lips with a red tongue.

"And now," said King, "I am going up into the forest to get some more fruit. It will be a light breakfast, but better than none; and I do not dare build up the fire again by daylight."

"While you are gone I shall bathe myself in the stream," said Fou-tan; "it will refresh me."

"I am afraid to leave you here alone," said King.

"There is no danger," replied Fou-tan. "The beasts are not hunting now, and there is little likelihood that the soldiers who are searching for us have broken camp so early. No, I shall remain here. Let me have my bath, Gordon King, and do not return too quickly."

As King walked down the gorge to the place where he could ascend into the forest, the brute upon the opposite side watched his every move and then proceeded quickly up the farther bank of the gorge in the opposite direction from that taken by King. There was no trail in the jungle that the brute did not know, so that he was aware of a place where he might easily descend into the gorge a short distance above the spot where Fou-tan bathed.

The girl wore only two garments beside her sandals—a silken sampot and the makeshift sarong—so that scarcely was King out of sight before she was splashing in the cold waters of the stream. The temperature of the water that came down from the high hills, coupled with her fear that King might return too soon, prompted her to haste. Having no towel, she used one end of the sarong to dry herself, adjusted her sampot and wound the sarong about her lithe body. Then she stood looking down the gorge in the direction from which King would return. Her heart was filled with her new happiness, so that it was with difficulty that she restrained her lips from song.

From up the gorge, behind her, crept the brute. Even if he had approached noisily, the rushing waters would have drowned the sound, but it was not the way of the brute to move noisily. Like the other carnivores, stealth was habitual to him. The brute was the personification of the cunning and malignity of the tiger; but there the parallel ceased, for the tiger was beautiful and the brute was hideous.

It is remarkable that there should be so many more beautiful creatures in the world than man, which suggests a doubt of man's boast that he is made in the image of God. There are those who believe that the image of God must transcend in its beauty the finite conceptions of man. If that be true and God chose to create any animal in His own likeness, man must have trailed at the far end of that celestial beauty contest.

The brute crept stealthily down upon the unsuspecting girl. He rounded the corner of a cliff and saw her standing with her back toward him. He moved swiftly now, crouched like a charging tiger, yet his naked feet gave forth no sound; while Fou-tan, with half-closed eyes and smiling lips, dreamed of the future that love held in store.

The brute sprang close behind her. A filthy, calloused paw was clapped across her mouth. A rough and powerful arm encircled her waist. She was whirled from her feet, her cries stifled in her throat, as the brute wheeled and ran swiftly up the gorge, bearing his prize.

King quickly found the fruit he sought, but he loitered in returning to give Fou-tan an opportunity to complete her toilet. As he idled slowly back to the gorge, his mind was occupied with plans for the future. He was considering the advisability of remaining in hiding where they were for several days on the chance that the soldiers of Lodivarman might in the meantime give up the search and return to Lodidha-pura. He determined that they might explore the gorge further in the hope of finding a safer and more comfortable retreat, where they might be less at the mercy of night prowlers and even more securely hidden from searchers than they were at present. He was also moved by the prospect of a few idyllic days during which there would be no one in the world but himself and Fou-tan.

Filled with enthusiasm for his heaven-sent plan, King descended into the gorge and approached the now hallowed precincts of his greatest happiness; but as he rounded the last bend he saw that Fou-tan was not there. Perhaps she had gone farther up the stream to bathe. He called her name aloud, but there was no reply. Again he called, raising his voice, but still there was only silence. Now he became alarmed and, running quickly forward, searched about for some sign or clue to her whereabouts; nor had he long to search. In the soft earth, damp from the recent rain, he saw the imprints of a huge foot—the great bare foot of a man. He saw where the prints had stopped and turned, and it was easy to follow them up the gorge. Casting aside the fruit that he had gathered, he hastened along the well-marked trail, his mind a fiery furnace of fear and rage, his heart a cold clod in his leaden breast.

Now, quite suddenly, he recalled the arrow he had found embedded behind the shoulders of the tiger that he had killed. He recalled the beast's sudden scream of rage and pain as it had charged so unexpectedly toward him, and quite accurately he reconstructed the whole scene—the man had been spying upon them from the top of the gorge; he had seen the tiger and had shot it to save his quarry to himself; then he had waited until King had left Fou-tan alone; the rest was plainly discernible in the footprints that he followed. He was confident that this was no soldier of Lodivarman; the crude arrow refuted that idea, as did the imprints of the great bare feet. But what sort of man was it and why had he stolen Fou-tan? The answer to that question goaded King to greater speed.

A short distance up the gorge King discovered where the tracks turned to the right, up the bed of a dry wash and thus to the level of the forest above. He gave thanks now for the providential rain that rendered the spoor easily followed. He knew that the abductor could not be far ahead, and he was sure that he could overtake him before harm could befall Fou-tan. However, as he hastened on, he was chilled by the thought that no matter how plain the spoor, the necessity for keeping it always in sight could but retard his speed; and his fear was that the slight delay might permit the man to outdistance him; and then he came to a patch of rocky ground where the trail, becoming immediately faint, suddenly disappeared entirely. Sick with apprehension, the American was forced to stop and search for a continuation of the tracks, and when, at last, he found them he knew that his quarry had gained greatly upon him during this enforced delay.

Again he sped along as rapidly as he could through a forest unusually devoid of underbrush. As he advanced he presently became aware of a new sound mingling with the subdued daylight noises of the jungle. It was a sound that he could not identify, but there was something ominous about it; and then, quite suddenly, he came upon the authors of it—great grey bulks looming among the boles of the trees directly in his path.

Under other circumstances he would have halted or, at least, changed his route; and had he reflected even for an instant, his better judgment now would have prompted him to do the latter; but uppermost in his mind and entirely dominating him was the great fear that he felt for Fou-tan's safety; and when he saw this obstacle looming menacingly before him, his one thought was to override it by sheer effrontery that it might not even delay him, much less thwart him in the pursuit of his object.

Had he been vouchsafed from his insanity even a single brief moment of lucidity, he would have avoided those ominous bulks moving restlessly to and fro among the boles of the giant trees, for even at the best wild elephants are nervous and short-tempered; and these, obviously disconcerted and suspicious by reason of some recent occurrences, were in a particularly hysterical and ugly mood. There were young calves among them and, therefore, watchful and irritable mothers; while the great bulls, aroused and on guard, were in no mood to be further provoked.

A huge bull, his ears outspread, his tail erect, wheeled toward the advancing man. The forest trembled to his mad trumpeting, and in that instant King realised for the first time the deadly peril of his position and knew that it would serve Fou-tan nothing were he to rush headlong into that inevitable death.

11

Warriors From Pnom Dhek

As the hideous creature bore her on, Fou-tan struggled to release herself; but she was utterly helpless in the Herculean grasp of her gigantic captor. She tried to wrench the creature's hand from her mouth that she might scream a warning to King, but even in this she was doomed to failure.

The creature had at first been carrying her under one arm, with her face down; but after he reached the floor of the forest he swung her lightly up in front of him, carrying her so that she had a clear view of his face; and at sight of it her heart sank within her. It was a hideous face, with thick lips and protruding teeth, great ears that flapped as the creature ran, and a low, receding forehead hidden by filthy, tangled hair that almost met the bushy, protruding eyebrows, beneath which gleamed wicked, bloodshot eyes.

It did not require a second look to convince Fou-tan that she had fallen into the hands of one of the dread Yeacks. Notwithstanding the fact that she had never before seen one of these ogre people, nor had known anyone who had, she was nevertheless as positive in her identification as though she had come in daily contact with them all her life, so strongly implanted in the mind of man are the superstitions of childhood. What else, indeed, could this creature be but a Yeack?

The horror of her situation was augmented by its contrast to the happy state from which it had snatched her. Had her Gordon King been there she would have been sure of rescue, so absolute was her conviction of his prowess. But how was he to know what had become of her? Being city-bred, it did not immediately occur to her that King might follow the tracks of her abductor, and so she was borne on more deeply into the sombre forest without even the slightly alleviating reassurance of faint hope. She was lost! Of that Fou-tan was convinced; for was it not well known that the Yeacks fed upon human flesh?

The brute, sensing muddily that he would be pursued, and having witnessed something of the prowess of King, did not pause in his flight but hastened steadily on toward a rocky fastness which he knew, where one might hide for days or, if discovered, find a cave, the mouth of which might be easily defended.

As he strode steadily through the forest his keen ears were presently attracted by a familiar sound, a sound which experience told him was a warning to change his course. A moment later he saw the elephants moving slowly across his path toward his left. He had no wish to dispute the right-of-way with them; so he veered to the right with the intention of passing behind them. They did not see him, but they caught his scent spoor, and an old bull left the herd and came ponderously down toward the point where the brute had first sighted them. The rest of the herd halted and then followed the old bull. The scent spoor of the man grated upon the nerves of the pachyderms. They became restless and irritable, more so because they could not locate the authors of this disturbing scent.

As the brute moved quickly to the right to circle to the rear of the herd and resume his interrupted course toward the wild sanctuary that was his objective, he kept his eyes turned to the left upon the members of the herd, lest, by chance, one of them might discover him and charge. A remote possibility, perhaps, but it is by guarding against remote possibilities that the fittest of primitive creatures survive. So, because of the fact that his attention was riveted in one direction, he did not see the danger approaching from another.

A score of soldiers, their brass cuirasses dulled and tarnished by the rain and dirt of jungle marches, halted at the sight of the brute and the burden he bore. A young officer in charge whispered a few low words of command. The soldiers crept forward, forming a half-circle as they went, to intercept the brute and his captive. One of the soldiers stumbled over a branch that had fallen from the tree above. Instantly the brute wheeled toward them. He saw twenty well-armed men advancing, their spears menacingly ready; and responding to the urge of Nature's first law, the brute cast the girl roughly to the ground and, wheeling, broke for freedom. A shower of arrows followed him and some of the soldiers would have pursued, but the officer called them back.

"We have the girl," he said; "let that thing go. We were not sent out for him. He is not the man who abducted the apsaras from the palace of Lodivarman."

At the moment that the brute had seen the soldiers, so had Fou-tan; and now she scrambled quickly to her feet, from where he had hurled her to the ground, and turned in flight back toward the gorge where she had last seen King.

"After her!" cried the officer; "but do not harm her."

Fou-tan ran fleetly and perhaps would have gotten away from them had not she tripped and fallen; as she scrambled to her feet, they were upon her. Rough hands seized her, but they did not harm her, nor did they offer her insult; for she who was to have been the favourite of Lodivarman might yet be, and it is not well to incur the displeasure of a king's favourite.

"Where is the man?" asked the officer, addressing Fou-tan.

The girl thought very quickly in that instant, and there was apparently no hesitation as she nodded her head in the direction that the fleeing brute had taken. "You know as well as I do," she said. "Why did you not capture him?"

"Not that man," said the officer. "I refer to the soldier of the guard who abducted you from the palace of Lodivarman."

"It was no soldier of the guard who abducted me," replied the girl. "This creature stole into the palace and seized me.

A soldier of the guard followed us into the jungle and tried to rescue me, but he failed.''

"Lodivarman sent word that it was the strange warrior, Gordon King, who stole you from the palace,'' said the officer.

"You saw the creature that stole me,'' said Fou-tan. "Did it look like a soldier of Lodivarman?''

"No,'' admitted the officer, "but where is this Gordon King? He has disappeared from Lodidhapura.''

"I told you that he tried to rescue me,'' explained Fou-tan. "He followed us into the jungle. What became of him I do not know. Perhaps the Yeacks wrought a magic spell that killed him.''

"Yeacks!'' exclaimed the officer. "What do you mean?''

"Did you not recognise my captor as a Yeack?'' asked Fou-tan. "Do you not know a Yeack when you see one?''

Exclamations arose from the soldiers gathered about them. "By the gods, it was a Yeack,'' said one. "Perhaps there are others about,'' suggested another. The man looked about them fearfully.

Fou-tan thought that she saw in their superstitious terror, which she fully shared herself, a possibility of escape. "The Yeacks will be angry with you for having taken me from one of their number,'' she said. "Doubtless he has gone to summon his fellows. You had best escape while you can. If you do not take me with you, they will not follow you.''

"By Siva, she is right!'' exclaimed a warrior.

"I am not afraid of the Yeacks,'' said the officer bravely; "but we have the apsaras and there is no reason why we should remain here longer. Come!'' He took Fou-tan gently by the arm.

"If you take me they will follow you,'' she said. "You had better leave me here.''

"Yes, leave her here,'' grumbled some of the warriors.

"We shall take the girl with us,'' said the officer. "I may escape the wrath of the Yeacks, but if I return to Lodidhapura without the apsaras I shall not escape the wrath of Lodivarman,'' and he gave the command to form for the march.

As the party moved away down toward the trail that leads to Lodidhapura, many were the nervous glances that the warriors cast behind them. There was much muttering and grumbling, and it was apparent that they did not relish being the escort of a recaptured prisoner of the Yeacks. Fou-tan fed their fears and their dissatisfaction by constant reference to the vengeance that would fall upon them in some form when the Yeacks should overtake them.

"You are very foolish to risk your life needlessly," she told the young officer. "If you leave me here you will be safe from the Yeacks, and no one in Lodidhapura need know that you have found me."

"Why should you wish to remain and become the victim of the Yeacks?" demanded the officer.

"It makes no difference whether you are with me or not," insisted Fou-tan. "The Yeacks will get me again. In some form they will come and take me. If you are with me they will slay you all."

"But there is a chance that we may escape them and get back to Lodidhapura," insisted the officer.

"I would rather remain with the Yeacks than go back to Lodivarman," said the girl. But in her breast was the hope that she could find Gordon King before the Yeacks overtook her; and, notwithstanding her superstitious fear of them, so great was her faith in the prowess of her man that she had no doubt but that he could overcome them.

Her arguments, however, were unavailing. She could not swerve the young officer from his determination to take her back to Lodidhapura. From the first however, it was apparent that the common soldiers were less enthusiastic about her company. The warriors of Pnom Dhek they could face with courage, or the charge of My Lord the Tiger, but contemplation of the supernatural powers of the mythological Yeacks filled their superstitious breasts with naught but terror. There were those among them who even discussed the advisability of murdering the officer, abandoning the girl, and returning to Lodidhapura with some plausible explanation, which their encounter with the Yeack readily suggested; but none of these things were they destined to do.

As King saw the great elephant advancing toward him he became seriously alive to the danger of his situation. He looked hurriedly about him, searching for an avenue of escape, but nowhere near was there a single tree of sufficient size to have withstood the titanic strength of the great bull should he have elected to fell it. To face the bull or to attempt to escape by running seemed equally futile; yet it was the latter alternative which commended itself to him as being the less suicidal.

But just then something happened. The bull stopped in his advance and looked suddenly toward his left. His trumpeting ceased, and then most unexpectedly he wheeled about and bolted directly away from King to be immediately followed by the entire herd, which went crashing through the jungle, bowling over trees in their mad progress until finally they disappeared from view.

With a sigh of relief King took up his interrupted pursuit, following in the wake of the elephants, which had disappeared in the direction taken by the abductor of Fou-tan. What had brought about the sudden change in the attitude of the bull King could not guess, nor did he ever discover. He attributed it to the mental vagaries of a naturally timid and nervous animal. He did not know that a changing breeze had brought to the nostrils of the pachyderm the scent spoor of many men—the soldiers of Lodivarman—nor was the matter of any particular importance to King, whose mind was occupied now with something of far greater moment. The stampeding elephants had entirely obliterated the tracks that King had been following, and this it was that gave him the greatest concern. It seemed that everything militated against the success of his pursuit. He zigzagged to the right and left of the elephant tracks in the hope of picking up the footprints of the fleeing man. When he had about abandoned hope, he saw in the soft earth a single familiar spoor—the imprint of a great flat foot. By what seemed little less than a miracle this single tell-tale clue had escaped the rushing feet of the herd. It pointed on in the direction that King had been going; and, with renewed hope, he hurried forward.

Among fallen trees, bowled over by the terrified elephants, King pursued his quarry until he was brought to a sudden stop by a tragic tableau of the jungle that instantly filled him with dire misgiving. A short distance ahead of him lay a man pinioned to the earth by a small tree that had fallen across his legs. Facing the man, crouching belly to the ground, advancing slowly inch by inch, was a great leopard. The man was helpless. In another instant the cat would be upon him, rending and tearing. Naturally the first thought that entered King's head was that this was the man who had abducted Fou-tan, and, if so, where was the girl? Until that question was answered the man must not die.

With a cry of warning intended to distract the attention of the leopard, King sprang forward, simultaneously fitting an arrow to his bow. The leopard leaped to its feet. For an instant it stood glaring menacingly at the advancing man; and seeing it hesitate, King did not launch his shaft, for he saw now that he might come within effective spear range of the beast before it charged; and he guessed that an arrow might only serve to infuriate it.

Disconcerted by this unexpected interference with its plans and with the interloper's bold advance, the brute hesitated a moment and then, wheeling, bounded off into the jungle.

The man lying upon the ground had been a witness to all this. He was saved from the leopard, but he looked apprehensively at King as the latter stopped beside him, for he recognised the newcomer as the man from whom he had stolen the girl. If he had any doubts as to the other's awareness of his guilt, it was dissipated by King's first words.

"Where is the girl?" demanded the American.

"The soldiers took her from me," replied the brute sullenly.

"What soldiers?"

"They were soldiers from Lodidhapura," replied the other.

"I believe that you are lying," said King, "and I ought to kill you." He raised his spear.

The brute did not wish to die. He had lost the girl, but he did not wish to lose his life also; and now, with effort, spurred by the desire to live, his brain gave birth to a simple idea. "You have saved my life," he said. "If you will raise this tree from my legs, I will help you to find the girl and take her away from the soldiers. That I will do if you do not kill me."

The man's spear had fallen beside him. As King considered the proposition he recovered the weapon and then took the bow and arrows from the man also.

"Why do you do that?" asked the brute.

"So that if I decide to release you, you may not be tempted to kill me," replied King.

"Very well," replied the brute, "but I shall not try to kill you." King stooped and seized the bole of the tree. It was not a very large tree, but it had fallen in such a way that the man, unassisted, could not have released himself; and as King raised it, the brute drew his legs from beneath it.

"Any bones broken?" asked King.

The brute rose slowly to his feet. "No," he said.

"Then let's be on our way," urged King. "We have no time to lose."

As the two men set out King walked a little in the rear of the other. He had been impressed from the first by the savage bestiality of his companion's face and now by his tremendous size. His huge, drooped shoulders and his long arms seemed capable of the most titanic feats of strength; yet the creature, who seemingly could have slain him as easily without weapons as with, led docilely on, until at last King was convinced that the fellow contemplated no treachery, but would carry out his part of the bargain with simple-minded loyalty.

"Who are you?" demanded King after they had walked in silence for a considerable distance.

"I am Prang," replied the brute.

"What were you doing out here in the jungle?" asked King.

"I live here," replied the brute.

"Where?"

"Anywhere," replied Prang with a broad gesture.

"Where are your people?" asked King.

"I have none; I live alone."

"Have you always lived in the jungle?"

"Not always, but for a long time."

"Where did you come from?"

"From Pnom Dhek."

"Then you are a runaway slave?" asked King.

The brute nodded his head. "But you need not try to return me. If you did that I should kill you."

"I do not intend to try to return you to Pnom Dhek. I am not from Pnom Dhek."

"Yes, I knew that from your armor," said the brute. "You are from Lodidhapura. You stole the girl and they sent soldiers after you. Is that not true?"

"Yes," replied King.

"It may be hard to take the girl away from the soldiers of Lodidhapura," said Prang. "We cannot do it by day, for they are many and we are few; but we can find them and follow them; and at night, perhaps, you can sneak into their camp and steal the girl, if she will come with you willingly."

"She will," said King; and then: "How long have you lived alone in the jungle, Prang?"

"I ran away when I was a boy. Many rains have come since then. I do not know how many, but it has been a long time."

As Prang led on through the jungle they conversed but little; enough, however, to assure King that the great, hulking brute had the mind of a little child, and as long as King did nothing to arouse his suspicions or his fears he would be quite docile and tractable. King noticed that Prang was not leading him back over the same route that they had come, and when he asked the man why they were going in a different direction, Prang explained that he knew the trail that the warriors would take in returning to Lodidhapura and that this was a short-cut to it.

In places the jungle was quite open and covered with tall, dry elephant grass, which, growing higher than their heads, obstructed their view in all directions, while the rustling of its leaves as they pushed their way through it drowned all other sounds. At such times King always felt particularly helpless and was relieved each time they emerged from the stifling embrace of the tall grasses; but Prang seemed not at all concerned, although he was walking almost naked and unarmed.

They had passed through a particularly long stretch of elephant grass when they emerged into a clearing entirely destitute of either grass or trees. Beyond the clearing, in front of them, they could see the forest at no great distance, but there was still a narrow belt of elephant grass which they must pass through before they reached the trees.

When they had advanced almost to the centre of this clearing, simultaneously their attention was attracted to a movement among the grasses ahead and to the left of them, and almost at the same moment a cuirassed soldier stepped into view, to be followed immediately by others. At the first glance King recognised that these men were not soldiers from Lodidhapura, for though their armour and harness were similar, they were not identical, and their helmets were of an entirely different pattern from that which he wore. At sight of them Prang halted, then he turned and started to run back in the direction from which they had come. ''Run!'' he cried, ''They are warriors from Pnom Dhek.''

Instantly King realised that these newcomers might prove to be Fou-tan's salvation if he could guide them to her, but without Prang that might be impossible, and therefore he turned and pursued the fleeing brute. Into the tall elephant grasses, close upon his heels, ran King. ''Stop!'' commanded the white man.

''Never!'' screamed Prang. ''They will take me back into slavery. Do not try to stop me, or I shall kill you.'' But the capture of Prang meant more to Gordon King than his life, and so he only redoubled his efforts to gain upon the fleeing man. Gradually he crept up upon him until at last he was within reach.

How futile it seemed to attempt to seize that mountain of muscle and bone, yet if he could detain him even momentarily he was positive that the soldiers would overtake them, for at the instant that they had turned to flee he had seen the soldiers from Pnom Dhek start in pursuit.

In King's experience he had learned but one way to stop a fleeing man without maiming or killing him, which he had no desire to do, although he held in his hands lethal weapons with which he might easily have brought down his quarry; and so he threw aside the spear that he carried and launched himself at the great legs of Prang. It was a noble tackle, and it brought Prang to earth with a resounding crash that almost knocked the wind out of him.

"Hurry!" yelled King to the soldiers of Pnom Dhek. "I have him!" He heard the warriors crashing through the dry grasses behind him.

"Let me go," cried the struggling Prang. "Let me go or they will take me back into slavery." But King clung to him in desperation, though it was much like attempting to cling to the business end of a mule, so mighty and vigorous were the kicks of Prang; and then the soldiers of Pnom Dhek arrived and fell upon both of them impartially.

"Don't kill him!" cried King as he saw the menacing spears of the warriors. "Wait until you hear me."

"Who are you?" demanded an officer. "What does this all mean? We saw you in company with this fellow; and now, though you are a soldier of Lodivarman, you turn upon your companion and capture him for us. What does it mean?"

"It is a long story," said King, "and there is no time for explanations now. Somewhere ahead of us there is a girl from Pnom Dhek whom I helped to escape from Lodidhapura. She has just been recaptured by some of Lodivarman's warriors. This man was guiding me to her. Will you help me to rescue this girl?"

"You are trying to lead me into a trap," said the officer suspiciously. "I do not believe that there is any girl."

"Yes, there is a girl," said Prang.

"Her name is Fou-tan," said King.

Interest was immediately evident in the eyes of the officer and excitement in the attitude of his men. "I will go with you," said the officer. "If you have lied to me and this is indeed a trap, you shall die at the first indication of treachery."

"I am content," said King; "but there is one more condition. I cannot lead you to the girl; but this man says that he can, and I know that he will do it willingly and quickly if you will promise him his freedom in return for his assistance."

A sudden gleam of hope shone in Prang's eyes as he heard King's words; and he looked up expectantly at the officer, awaiting his reply.

"Certainly," said the latter. "If he leads us to Fou-tan, he shall have not only his liberty but any other reward that he may desire. I can promise him that."

"I wish only my freedom," said Prang.

"Lead on, then," said the officer. And then as the march started he detailed two warriors to remain constantly at Prang's side and two with King, and these warriors he instructed to kill their charges at the first indication of treachery.

Evidently interested in King, the officer walked beside him. It was apparent that he had noticed the lack of physical resemblance to the Khmers and his curiosity was aroused. "You do not greatly resemble the men of Lodidhapura," he said finally.

"I am not of Lodidhapura," said King.

"But you are in the armour of Lodivarman's warriors," insisted the officer.

"I am from a far country," explained King. "Lost in the jungle, I was taken prisoner by Lodivarman's warriors. I pleased the King, and he gave me service in the royal guard."

"But how is it, then, that you are befriending a girl from Pnom Dhek?"

"That, as I told you, is a long story," said King, "but

when we have found her she will corroborate all that I have said. I was forced into the service of Lodivarman. I owe him no loyalty, and should I fall into his hands again I can expect no mercy. Therefore, it had been my intention, when I reached Pnom Dhek with Fou-tan, to seek service in your army.''

''If you have befriended Fou-tan, your petition will not go unheeded,'' said the officer.

''You have heard of her, then?'' asked King.

The officer gave the American a long, searching look before he replied. ''Yes,'' he said.

12

※

Guest and Prisoner

The captors of Fou-tan were exerting no effort to make haste. For almost two days they had been marching rapidly through the jungle, searching for a clue to the whereabouts of Fou-tan and her escort; and now that they had found her, they were taking it easy, moving slowly toward the spot where they were to camp for the night. Knowing nothing of the presence of the soldiers of Beng Kher of Pnom Dhek, they anticipated no pursuit. Their conversation was often filled with conjecture as to the identity of Fou-Tan's companion. Some of them insisted that the Yeack and King were one and the same.

"I always knew that there was something wrong with the fellow," opined a warrior; "there was a peculiar look about him. He was no Khmer; nor was he of any race of mortal men."

"Perhaps he was a Naga, who took the form first of a man and then changed himself into a Yeack," suggested another.

"I think that he was a Yeack all along," said another, "and that he took the form of man only to deceive us, that he might enter the palace of Lodivarman and steal the girl."

It was while they were discussing this matter that a warrior marching at the rear of the column was attracted by a noise behind him. Turning his head to look, he gave a sudden cry of alarm, for in their rear, creeping upon them, he saw the brute and a body of soldiers.

"The Yeacks are coming!" he cried.

The others turned quickly at his warning cry. "I told you so," screamed one. "The Yeack has brought his fellows."

"Those are soldiers of Pnom Dhek," cried the officer. "Form line and advance upon them. Let it not be said that men of Lodidhapura fled from the warriors of Beng Kher."

"They are Yeacks who have taken the form of soldiers of Pnom Dhek," cried a warrior. "Mortals cannot contend against them," and with that he threw down his spear and fled.

At the same instant the soldiers of Pnom Dhek leaped forward, shouting their war-cry.

The defection of the single Lodidhapurian warrior was all that had been needed to ignite the smouldering embers of discontent and mutiny already fully fed by their superstitious fears. To a man, the common soldiers turned and ran, leaving their officer and Fou-tan alone. For an instant the man stood his ground and then, evidently realising the hopelessness of his position, he, too, wheeled and followed his retreating men at top speed.

What Fou-tan's feelings must have been, it was difficult to imagine. Here, suddenly and entirely without warning, appeared a company of soldiers from her native city, and with them were the horrid Yeack that had stolen her away from King and also Gordon King himself. For a moment she stood in mute and wide-eyed wonderment as the men approached her, and then she turned to the man she loved. "Gordon King," she said, "I knew that you would come."

The soldiers of Pnom Dhek gathered around her, the common warriors keeping at a respectful distance, while the officer approached and, kneeling, kissed her hand.

King was not a little puzzled for an explanation of the evident respect in which they held her, but then he realised that he was not familiar with the customs of the country. He was aware, however, that the apsarases, or dancing girls of the temples, were held in considerable veneration because of the ritualistic nature of their dances, which identified them closely with the religious life of the nation and rendered them, in a way, the particular wards of the gods.

The officer questioned her briefly and respectfully; and, having thus assured himself of King's loyalty and integrity, his attitude toward the American changed from suspicion to cordiality.

To Fou-tan's questions relative to Prang, King explained by telling the story of the brute as he had had it from his own lips; yet it was evidently most difficult for Fou-tan to relinquish her conviction that the creature was a Yeack; nor could any other have assured her of Prang's prosaic status than Gordon King, in whose lightest words she beheld both truth and authority.

"Now that I have led you to the girl," said Prang, addressing the officer, "give me the liberty that you promised me."

"It is yours," said the officer; "but if you wish to return and live in Pnom Dhek I can promise you that the King will make you a free man."

"Yes," said Fou-tan, "and you shall have food and clothing as long as you live."

The brute shook his head. "No," he said. "I am afraid of the city. Let me stay in the jungle, where I am safe. Give me back my weapons and let me go."

They did as he requested, and a moment later Prang slouched off into the forest soon to be lost to their view, choosing the freedom of the jungle to the luxuries of the city.

Once again the march was resumed, this time in the direction of Pnom Dhek. As Fou-tan and King walked side by side the girl said to him in a low voice, "Do not let them know yet of our love. First, I must win my father, and after that the whole world may know."

All during the long march King was again and again impressed by the marked deference accorded Fou-tan. It was so noticeable that the natural little familiarities of their own comradeship took on the formidable aspects of sacrilege by comparison. To King's western mind it seemed strange that so much respect should be paid to a temple dancing girl; but he was glad that it was so, for in his heart he knew that whatever reverence they showed Fou-tan she deserved, because of the graces of her character and the purity of her soul.

The long march to Pnom Dhek was uneventful, and near the close of the second day the walls of the city rose before them across a clearing as they emerged from the forest. In outward appearance Pnom Dhek was similar to Lodidhapura. Its majestic piles of masonry arose in stately grandeur above the jungle. Its ornate towers and splendid temples bore witness to the wealth and culture of its builders, and over all was the same indefinable suggestion of antiquity. Pnom Dhek was a living city, yet so softened and mellowed by the passing centuries that even in life it suggested more the reincarnation of ancient glories than an actuality of the present.

"Pnom Dhek!" whispered Fou-tan, and in her tone there were love and reverence.

"You are glad to get back?" asked King.

"That can scarcely express what I feel," replied the girl. "I doubt if you can realise what Pnom Dhek means to one of her sons or daughters; and so, too, you cannot guess the gratitude that I feel to you, Gordon King, who, alone are responsible for my return."

He looked at her for a moment in silence. As she stood devouring Pnom Dhek with her eyes there was a rapturous exaltation in her gaze that suggested the fervour of religious passion, and the thought gave him pause.

"Perhaps, Fou-tan," he suggested, "you have mistaken gratitude for love."

She looked up at him quickly. "You do not understand, Gordon King," she said. "For two thousand years love for Pnom Dhek has been bred into the blood that animates me. It is a part of me that can die only when I die; yet I could never see Pnom Dhek again and yet be happy; though should I never see you again, I might never be happy again even in Pnom Dhek. Now do you understand?"

"That I was jealous of stone and wood shows how much I love you, Fou-tan," he said.

A soldier, lightened of his cuirass and weapons, had run swiftly ahead to the city gates, which they were approaching, to announce their coming; and presently there was a blare of trumpets at the gate, and this was answered by the sound of other trumpets within the city and the deep booming of gongs and the ringing of bells until the whole city was alive with noise. Then once again was King mystified; but there was more to come.

As they moved slowly now along the avenue toward the city gates, a company of soldiers emerged and behind them a file of elephants, gaudily trapped, and surging forward upon either side of these were people—men, women and children—shouting and singing, until from hundreds their numbers grew to thousands. So quickly had they gathered that it seemed as much a miracle to King as did the occasion for their rejoicing, and now he became convinced that Fou-tan must be a priestess at least, if all this rejoicing and pandemonium were in honour of her return.

The populace, outstripping the soldiers, were the first to reach them. Quickly the warriors that composed their escort formed a ring about Fou-tan and King, but the people held their distance respectfully, and now out of the babel of voices King caught some of the words of their greeting—words that filled him with surprise.

"Fou-tan! Fou-tan!" they cried. "Welcome to our beloved Princess that was lost and is found again!"

King turned to the girl. "Princess!" he exclaimed. "You did not tell me, Fou-tan."

"Many men have courted me because I am a princess," she said. "You loved me for myself alone, and I wanted to cling to that as long as I might."

"And Beng Kher is your father?" he asked.

"Yes, I am the daughter of the King," replied Fou-tan.

"I am glad that I did not know," said King simply.

"And so am I," replied the girl, "for now no one can ever make me doubt your love."

"I wish that you were not a princess," he said in a troubled voice.

"Why?" she demanded.

"None would have objected had the slave girl wished to marry me," he said, "but I can well imagine that many will object to a nameless warrior taking the Princess of Pnom Dhek.''

"Perhaps,'' she said sadly, "but let us not think of that now.''

In the howdah of the leading elephant sat a large, stern-faced man, beneath a parasol of cloth of gold and red. When the elephant upon which he rode was stopped near them, ladder-like steps were brought from the back of an elephant in the rear and the man descended to the ground, while the people prostrated themselves and touched their foreheads to the earth. As the man approached, Fou-tan advanced to meet him, and when she was directly in front of him, she kneeled and took his hand. There was moisture in the man's stern eyes as he lifted the girl to her feet and took her into his arms. It was Beng Kher the King, father of Fou-tan.

After the first greeting Fou-tan whispered a few words to Beng Kher, and immediately Beng Kher directed Gordon King to advance. Following Fou-tan's example, the American knelt and kissed the King's hand. "Arise!'' said Beng Kher. "My daughter, the Princess, tells me that it is to you she owes her escape from Lodidhapura. You shall be suitably rewarded. You shall know the gratitude of Beng Kher.'' He signalled to one of his retinue that had descended from the elephant in his rear. "See that this brave warrior lacks for nothing,'' he said. "Later we shall summon him to our presence again.''

Once more did Fou-tan whisper a few low words to her father, the King.

The King knit his brows as though he were not entirely pleased with whatever suggestion Fou-tan had made, but presently the lines of his face softened and again he turned to the official to whom he had just spoken. "You will conduct the warrior to the palace and accord him all honour, for he is to be the guest of Beng Kher.'' Then, with Fou-tan, he ascended into the howdah of the royal elephant, while the officer, whom he had designated to escort Gordon King, approached the American.

King's first impression of the man was not a pleasant one.

The fellow's face was coarse and sensual and his manner haughty and supercilious. He made no attempt to conceal his disgust as his eyes appraised the soiled and tarnished raiment of the common warrior before him. "Follow me, my man," he said. "The King has condescended to command that you be quartered in the palace," and without further words of greeting he turned and strode toward the elephant upon which he had ridden from the city.

In the howdah with them were two other gorgeously dressed officials and a slave who held a great parasol over them all. With no consideration for his feelings and quite as though he had not been present, King's companions discussed the impropriety of inviting a common soldier to the palace. Suddenly his escort turned toward him. "What is your name, my man?" he demanded, arrogantly.

"My name is Gordon King," replied the American; "but I am not your man." His voice was low and even and his level gaze was directed straight into the eyes of the officer.

The man's eyes shifted and then he flushed and scowled. "Perhaps you do not know," he said, "that I am the prince, Bharata Rahon." His tone was supercilious, his voice unpleasant.

"Yes?" inquired King politely. So this was Bharata Rahon—this was the man whom Beng Kher had selected as the husband of Fou-tan. "No wonder she ran away and hid in the jungle," murmured King.

"What is that?" demanded Bharata Rahon. "What did you say?"

"I am sure," said King, "that the noble prince would not be interested in anything a common warrior might say."

Bharata Rahon grunted and the conversation ended; nor did either address the other again as the procession wound its way through the avenues of Pnom Dhek toward the palace of the King. The way was lined with cheering people, and strongly apparent to King was the sincerity of their welcome to Fou-tan and the reality of their happiness that she had been returned to them.

The palace of Beng Kher was a low rambling building

covering a considerable area. Its central portion had evidently been conceived as a harmonious unit, to which various kings had added without much attention to harmony; yet the whole was rather impressive and was much larger than the palace of Lodivarman. The grounds surrounding it were beautifully planted and maintained with meticulous care. The gate through which they passed into the royal enclosure was of great size and had evidently been designed to permit the easy passage of a column of elephants, two abreast.

The avenue from the gate led straight between old trees to the main entrance to the palace, and here the party descended from their howdahs and followed in the train of Beng Kher and Fou-tan as they entered the palace amidst such pomp and ceremony as King never before had witnessed. It occurred to him that if such things must follow the comings and goings of kings, the glory of sovereignty had decided drawbacks. There were at least two hundred soldiers, functionaries, courtiers, priests, and slaves occupied with the ceremony of receiving the King and the Princess into the palace, and with such mechanical accuracy did they take their posts and perform their parts that it was readily apparent to the American that they were observing a formal custom to which they had become accustomed by long and continued usage.

Down a long corridor, those in the royal party followed Beng Kher and Fou-tan to a large audience chamber, where the King dismissed them. Then he passed on through a doorway with Fou-tan; and when the door closed behind them, most of the party immediately dispersed.

Bharata Rahon beckoned King to follow him and, conducting him to another part of the palace, led him into a room which was one of a suite of three.

"Here are your quarters," said Bharata Rahon. "I shall send slaves with apparel more suitable for the guest of Beng Kher. Food will be served to you here. Do not leave the apartment until you receive instructions from the King or from me."

"I thought that I was a guest," said King, "but it appears that I am a prisoner."

"That is as the King wills," replied the prince. "You should be more grateful, fellow, for the favours that you already have received."

"Phew!" exclaimed King as Bharata Rahon left the room. "It is certainly a relief to get rid of you. The more I see of you the easier it is to understand how Fou-tan preferred My Lord the Tiger to Prince Bharata Rahon."

As King examined the rooms assigned to him, he saw that they overlooked the royal garden at a particularly beautiful spot; nor could he wonder now why Fou-tan loved her home.

His reveries were interrupted by the coming of two slaves; one carried warm water for a bath, and the other raiment suitable for a king's guest. They told him that they had been assigned to serve him while he remained in the palace and that one of them would always be in attendance, remaining in the corridor outside his door. The water, which was contained in two earthen vessels and supported at the ends of a pole that one of the slaves carried across his shoulders, was taken to the innermost of the three rooms and deposited beside a huge earthen bowl that was so large that a man might sit down inside it. Towels and brushes were brought and other necessary requisites of the toilet.

King stripped and entered the bowl, and then one of the slaves poured water over him while the other scrubbed him vigorously with two brushes. It was, indeed, a heroic bath, but it left King stimulated and exhilarated and much refreshed after his tiresome journey.

The scrubbing completed to their satisfaction, they bade him step out of the bowl on to a soft rug, where they oiled his body from head to foot and then proceeded to rub his skin vigorously until all of the oil had disappeared. Following this, they anointed him with some sweet-smelling lotion; and while the water-carrier emptied the bowl and carried the bath water away, the other slave assisted King as he donned his new clothing.

"I am Hamar," whispered the fellow after the other slave had left the apartment. "I belong to Fou-tan, who trusts me. She sent this to you as a sign that you may trust me also."

He handed King a tiny ring, a beautiful example of the gold-smith's art. It was strung upon a golden chain. "Wear it about your neck," said Hamar. "It will take you in safety many places in Pnom Dhek. Only the King's authority is greater than this."

"Did she send no message?" asked King.

"She said to tell you that all was not as favourable as she had hoped, but to be of good heart."

"Convey my thanks to her if you can," said King, "and tell her that her message and her gift have cheered me."

The other slave returned now, and as King had no further need of them, he dismissed them both.

The two had scarcely departed when a young man entered, resplendent in the rich trappings of an officer.

"I am Indra Sen," announced the new-comer. "Bharata Rahon has sent me to see that you do not lack for entertainment in the palace of Beng Kher."

"Bharata Rahon did not seem to relish the idea of entertaining a common warrior," said King with a smile.

"No," replied the young man. "Bharata Rahon is like that. Sometimes he puts on such airs that one might think him the King himself. Indeed, he has hopes some day of becoming king, for it is said that Beng Kher would marry Fou-tan to him, and as Beng Kher has no son, Fou-tan and Bharata Rahon would rule after Beng Kher died, which may the gods forbid."

"Forbid that Beng Kher die?" asked King; "or that Fou-tan and Bharata Rahon rule?"

"There is none but would serve Fou-tan loyally and gladly," replied Indra Sen; "but there is none who likes Bharata Rahon, and it is feared that as Fou-tan's husband he might influence her to do things which she would not otherwise do."

"It is strange," said King, "that Beng Kher has no son in a land where a king takes many wives."

"He has many sons," replied Indra Sen, "but the son of a concubine may not become king. Beng Kher would take but one queen, and when she died he would have no other."

"If Fou-tan had not been found and Beng Kher had died, would Bharata Rahon have become king?" asked the American.

"In that event the princes would have chosen a new king, but it would not have been Bharata Rahon," replied the officer.

"Then his only hope of becoming king is by marrying Fou-tan?"

"That is his only hope."

"And Beng Kher favours his suit?" continued King.

"The man seems to exercise some strange influence over Beng Kher," explained Indra Sen. "The King's heart is set upon wedding Fou-tan to him, and because the King is growing old he would have this matter settled quickly. It is well known that Fou-tan objects. She does not want to marry Bharata Rahon, but though the King indulges her in every other whim, he is adamant in this matter. Once Fou-tan ran away into the jungle to escape the marriage; and no one knows yet what the outcome will be, for our little princess, Fou-tan, has a will and a mind of her own; but the King—well, he is the King."

For three days Indra Sen performed the duties of a host. He conducted King about the palace grounds; he took him to the temples and out into the city, to the market place, and the bazaars. Together they watched the apsarases dance in the temple court; but during all this time King saw nothing of Fou-tan, nor did Beng Kher send for him. Twice he had received brief messages from Fou-tan through Hamar, but they were only such messages as might be transmitted by word of mouth through a slave and were far from satisfying the man's longing for his sweetheart.

Upon the fourth day Indra Sen did not come, as was his custom, early in the morning; nor did Hamar appear, but only the other slave—an ignorant, taciturn man whom King never had been able to engage in conversation.

King had never left his apartment except in the company of Indra Sen, and while Bharata Rahon had warned him against any such independent excursion the American had not taken the suggestion seriously, believing it to have been animated solely by the choler of the Khmer prince. Heretofore, Indra Sen had arrived before there might be any occasion for King to wish to venture forth alone; but there had never been anything in the attitude of the young officer to indicate that the American was other than an honoured guest, nor had there been any reason to believe that he might not come and go as he chose. Having waited, therefore, for a considerable time upon Indra Sen on this particular morning, King decided to walk out into the royal garden after leaving word with the slave, who always attended just outside his door, that the young officer, when he came, might find him there; but when he opened the door into the corridor there was no slave, but, instead, two burly warriors, who instantly turned and barred the exit with their spears.

"You may not leave your quarters," said one of them gruffly and with a finality that seemed to preclude argument.

"And why not?" demanded the American. "I am the King's guest and I only wish to walk in the garden."

"We have received our orders," replied the warrior. "You are not permitted to leave your quarters."

"Then it would appear that I am not the King's guest, but the King's prisoner."

The warrior shrugged. "We have our orders," he said; "other than this we know nothing."

The American turned back into the room and closed the door. What did it all mean? He crossed the apartment to one of the windows and stood looking out upon the garden. He rehearsed his every act and speech since he had entered Pnom Dhek, searching for some clue that might explain the change of attitude toward him; but he found nothing that might warrant it; and so he concluded that it was the result of something that had occurred of which he had no knowledge; but the natural inference was that it was closely allied to his love for Fou-tan and Beng Kher's determination that she should wed Bharata Rahon.

The day wore on. The taciturn slave came with food, but Hamar did not appear; nor did Indra Sen. King paced his

quarters like a caged tiger. Always the windows overlooking
the garden attracted him, so that often he paused before them,
drawn by the freedom which the garden suggested in contrast
to the narrow confines of his quarters. For the thousandth
time he examined the quarters that had now become his
prison. The paintings and hangings that covered the leaden
walls had always aroused his interest and curiosity; but to-
day, by reason of constant association, he found them palling
upon him. The familiar scenes depicting the activities of kings
and priests and dancing girls, the stiffly delineated warriors
whose spears never cast and whose bolts were never shot
oppressed him now. Their actions for ever inhibited and imprisoned in the artist's paint suggested his own helpless state
of imprisonment.

The sun was sinking in the west; the long shadows of the
parting day were creeping across the royal garden of Beng
Kher; the taciturn slave had come with food and had lighted
lamps in each of the three rooms of his apartment—crude
wick floating in oil they were, but they served to dispel the
darkness of descending night. King, vibrant with the vitality
of youth and health, had eaten heartily. The slave removed
the dishes and returned.

"Have you further commands for the night, master?" he
asked.

King shook his head. "No," he said, "you need not return until the morning."

The slave withdrew, and King fell to playing with an idea
that had been slowly forming in his mind. The sudden change
in his status here that had been suggested by the absence of
Hamar and Indra Sen and by the presence of the warriors in
the corridor had aroused within him a natural apprehension
of impending danger, and consequently directed his mind
toward thoughts of escape.

The windows not far above the garden, the darkness of the
night, his knowledge of the city and the jungle—all impressed upon him the belief that he might win to freedom
with no considerable risk; yet he was still loath to make the
attempt because as yet he had nothing definite upon which

to base his suspicion that the anger of Beng Kher had been turned upon him, and further, and more important still, because he could not leave Pnom Dhek without first having word with Fou-tan.

As he inwardly debated these matters he paced to and fro the length of the three rooms of his apartment. He had paused in the innermost of the three where the flickering light of the cresset projected his shadow grotesquely upon an ornate hanging that depended from the ceiling to the floor. He had paused there in deep thought, his eyes, seeing and yet unseeing, fastened upon this splendid fabric, when suddenly he saw it move and bulge. There was something or someone behind it.

13

※

Farewell For Ever!

For the first time since Gordon King had entered the palace of Beng Kher as a guest he was confronted with the realisation that the ornate apparel and trappings that had been furnished him had included no weapons of defence; and now as he saw the hanging bulging mysteriously before his eyes he stepped quickly toward it, prepared to meet either friend or foe with his bare hands. He saw the bulging fold move slowly behind the fabric toward its outer edge, and he followed, ready for any eventuality. With a quick movement the margin of the fabric was pulled aside as Hamar, the slave, stepped into the room, and at the same instant King seized him by the throat.

Recognition was instantaneous and, with a smile, the American released the slave and stepped back. "I did not know whom to expect, Hamar," he said.

"You were well to be prepared for an enemy, master," said the slave in low tones, "for you have powerful ones in Pnom Dhek."

"What brings you here, Hamar, in secrecy and in such mystery?" demanded King.

"Are you alone?" asked Hamar in a whisper.

"Yes."

"Then my mission is fulfilled," said Hamar. "I do but ensure the safety and the secrecy of another who follows me."

Again the hanging bulged as someone passed behind it; and an instant later Fou-tan stood before Gordon King, while the slave, Hamar, bowing low, withdrew.

"Fou-tan!" exclaimed Gordon King, taking a step toward the girl.

"My Gordon King!" whispered Fou-tan as his arms closed about her.

"What has happened that you come to me in this way?" asked King. "I knew that there was something wrong because neither Hamar nor Indra Sen came to-day and there were warriors posted at my door to keep me prisoner. But why talk of such things when I have you? Nothing else counts now, my Fou-tan."

"Ah, Gordon King, but there *is* much else that counts," replied the girl. "I should have come before, but guards were placed to keep me from you. The King, my father, is mad with rage. To-morrow you are to be destroyed."

"But why?" demanded King.

"Because yesterday I went to my father and confessed our love. I appealed to his gratitude to you for having saved me from Lodivarman and to his love for me, believing that these might outweigh his determination to wed me to Bharata Rahon, but I was mistaken. He flew into an uncontrollable rage of passion. He ordered me to my apartment and he commanded that you be destroyed upon the morrow; but I found a way, thanks to Hamar and Indra Sen, and so I have come to bid you farewell, Gordon King, and to tell you that wherever you may go my heart goes with you, though my body may be the unwilling slave of another. Indra Sen and Hamar will guide you to the jungle and point the way toward the great river that lies in the direction of the rising sun, upon whose opposite shore you will be safe from the machination of Beng Kher and Bharata Rahon."

"And you, Fou-tan—you will go with me?"

The girl shook her head. "No, Gordon King, I may not," she replied sadly.

"And why?" he asked. "You love me and I love you. Come away with me into a land of freedom and happiness, where no one will question our right to love and to live as the gods intended that we should; for you, Fou-tan, and I were made for one another."

"It cannot be, Gordon King," replied the girl. "The thing that you suggest offers to me the only happiness that can be possible to me in life, but for such as I there is an obligation that transcends all thoughts of personal happiness. I was born a princess, and because of that there have devolved upon me certain obligations which may not be escaped. Had I brothers or sisters born of a queen it might be different, but through me alone may the royal dynasty of Pnom Dhek be perpetuated. No, Gordon King, not even love may intervene between a princess of Pnom Dhek and her duty to her people. Always shall my love be yours, and it will be harder for me than for you. If I, who am weak, am brave because of duty, how can you, a man, be less brave? Kiss me once more, then, and for the last time, Gordon King; then go with Hamar and Indra Sen, who will lead you to the jungle and point the way to safety."

As she ceased speaking she threw her arms about his neck and drew his lips to hers. He felt her tears upon his cheeks, and his own eyes grew dim. Perhaps not until this instant of parting had King realised the hold that this dainty flower of the savage jungle had taken upon his heart. As fragile and beautiful as the finest of Meissen ceramics, this little, painted princess of a long dead past held him in a bondage beyond the power of steel.

"I cannot give you up, Fou-tan," he said. "Let me remain. Perhaps if I talked with your father—"

"It would be useless," she said, "even if he would grant you an audience, which he will not."

"Then if you love me as I love you," said King, "you will come away with me."

"Do not say that, Gordon King. It is cruel," replied the girl. "I am taught to place duty above all other considerations, even love. Princesses are not born to happiness. Their exalted birth dedicates them to duty. They are more than human, and so human happiness often is denied them. And now you must go. Indra Sen and Hamar are waiting to guide you to safety. Each moment of delay lessens your chances for escape."

"I do not wish to escape," said King. "I shall remain and face whatever consequences are in store for me, for without you, Fou-tan, life means nothing to me. I would rather remain and die than go away without you."

"No, no," she cried. "Think of me. I must live on, and always, if I believe you to be alive, I shall be happier than I could be if I knew that you were dead."

"You mean that if I were alive there still would be hope?" he asked.

She shook her head. "Not in the way you mean," she replied; "but there would be happiness for me in knowing that perhaps somewhere you were happy. For my sake, you must go. If you love me you will not deny me this shred of happiness."

"If I go," he said, "you will know that wherever I am, I am unhappy."

"I am a woman as well as a princess," she replied, "and so perhaps it will give me a sad happiness to know that you are unhappy because I am denied you." She smiled ruefully.

"Then I shall go, Fou-tan, if only to make you happy in my unhappiness; but I think that I shall not go far and that always I shall nurse hope in my breast, even though you may have put it from you. Think of me, then, as being always near you, Fou-tan, awaiting the day when I may claim you."

"That will never be, Gordon King," she replied sadly; "yet it will do no harm if in our hearts we nurse a hopeless hope. Kiss me again. It is Fou-tan's last kiss of love."

An eternity of love and passion were encompassed in that brief instant of their farewell embrace, and then Fou-tan tore herself from his arms and was gone.

She was gone! King stood for a long time gazing at the hanging that had moved for a moment to the passage of her lithe figure. It did not seem possible that she had gone out of his life for ever. "Fou-tan!" he whispered. "Come back to me. You will come back!" But the dull pain in his breast was his own best answer to the anguished cry of his stricken soul.

Again the hanging moved and bulged, and his heart leaped to his throat; but it was only Hamar, the slave.

"Come, master!" cried the man. "There is no time to be lost."

King nodded. With leaden steps he followed Hamar to an opening in the wall behind the hanging, and there he found Indra Sen in the mouth of a corridor, a flickering torch in his hand.

"In the service of the Princess," said the officer.

"May the gods protect her and give her every happiness," replied King.

"Come!" said Indra Sen, and turning he led the way along the corridor and down a long flight of stone steps that King knew must lead far beneath the palace. They passed the mouths of branching corridors, attesting the labyrinthine maze that honeycombed the earth beneath the palace of Beng Kher, and then the tunnel led straight and level out beneath the city of Pnom Dhek to the jungle beyond.

"That way lies the great river, Gordon King," said Indra Sen, pointing toward the east. "I should like to go with you farther, but I dare not; if Hamar and I are suspected of aiding in your escape, the blame may be placed upon the Princess, since Hamar is her slave and I an officer of her guard."

"I would not ask you to go farther, Indra Sen," replied King, "nor can I find words in which to thank either you or Hamar."

"Here, master," said Hamar, "is the clothing that you wore when you came to Pnom Dhek. It will be more suitable in the jungle than that you are wearing," and he handed King a bundle that he had been carrying. "Here, also, are weapons—a spear, a knife, a bow and arrows. They are gifts from the Princess, who says that no other knows so well how to use them."

The two waited until King had changed into his worn trappings, and then, bidding him good-bye, they entered the mouth of the tunnel, leaving him alone in the jungle. To the east lay the Mekong, where he might construct a raft and drift down to civilisation. To the south lay Lodidhapura, and beyond that the dwelling of Che and Kangrey. King knew that if he went to the east and the Mekong he would never return. He thought of Susan Anne Prentice and his other friends of the outer world; he thought of the life of usefulness that lay ahead of him there. Then there came to him the vision of a dainty girl upon a great elephant, reminding him of that moment, now so long ago, that he had first seen Fou-tan; and he knew that he must choose now, once and for all, between civilisation and the jungle—between civilisation and the definite knowledge that he would never see her again or the jungle and hope, however remote.

"Susan Anne would think me a fool, and I am quite sure that she would be right," he murmured, as with a shrug he turned his face squarely toward the south and set off upon his long and lonely journey through the jungle.

In his mind there was no definite plan beyond a hazy determination to return to Che and Kangrey and to remain there with them until it would be safe to assume that Beng Kher had ceased to search for him. After that, perhaps, he might return to the vicinity of Pnom Dhek. And who could say what might happen then? Thus strongly is implanted in the breast of man the eternal seed of hope. Of course, he knew that he was a fool, but it did not displease him to be a fool if his foolishness kept him in the same jungle with Fou-tan.

The familiar odours and noises of the jungle assailed his nostrils and his ears. With spear in readiness he groped his way to the trail which he knew led toward the south and his destination. When he found it, some caprice of hope prompted him to blaze a tree at the spot in such a way that he might easily identify it, should he chance to come upon it again.

All night he travelled. Once, for a long time, he knew that some beast was stalking him; but if it had evil intentions toward him it evidently could not muster the courage to put them into action, for eventually he heard it no more. Shortly thereafter dawn came and with it a sense of greater security.

Shortly after sunrise he came upon a herd of wild pigs, and before they were aware of his presence he had sunk an arrow into the heart of a young porker. Then an old boar discovered him and charged, its gleaming tusks flecked with foam, its savage eyes red-rimmed with rage; but King did not wait to discuss matters with the great beast. Plentiful and inviting about him grew the great trees of the jungle, and into one of these he swung himself as the boar tore by.

The rest of the herd had disappeared; but for a long time the boar remained in the vicinity, trotting angrily back and forth along the trail beneath King and occasionally stopping to glare up at him malevolently. It seemed an eternity to the hungry man, but at length the boar appeared to realise the futility of waiting longer for his prey to descend and trotted off into the jungle after his herd, the sound of his passage through the underbrush gradually diminishing until it was lost in the distance. Then King descended and retrieved his kill. Knowing the cunning of savage tuskers of the jungle, King was aware that the boar might return to the spot; and so he did not butcher his kill there, but, throwing it across his shoulder, continued on for about a mile. Then, finding a suitable location he stopped and built a fire, over which he soon was grilling a generous portion of his quarry.

After eating, he left the trail and, going into the jungle a short distance, found a place where he could lie down to sleep; and as he dozed he dreamed of snowy linen and soft pillows and heard the voices of many people arguing and scolding. They annoyed him, so that he determined to sell his home and move to another neighbourhood; and then seemingly in the same instant he awoke, though in reality he had slept for six hours. Uppermost in his mind was his complaint against his neighbours, and loud in his ears were their voices as he opened his eyes and looked around in puzzled astonishment at the jungle about him. Then he smiled as the dream picture of his home faded into the reality of his surroundings. The smile broadened into a grin as he caught sight of the monkeys chattering and scolding in the tree above him.

Another night he pushed on through the jungle, and as morning came he guessed that he must be approaching the vicinity of Lodidhapura. He made no kill that morning and built no fire, but satisfied himself with fruits and nuts, which he found in abundance. He had no intention of risking discovery and capture by attempting to pass Lodidhapura by day, and so he found a place where he could lie up until night.

This time he dreamed of Fou-tan and it was a pleasant dream, for they were alone together in the jungle and all obstacles had been removed from their path, but presently they heard people approaching; they seemed to be all about them, and their presence and their talk annoyed Fou-tan and angered King; in fact, he became so angry that he awoke. As the figure of Fou-tan faded from his side, he kept his eyes tight shut, trying to conjure her back again; but the voices of the intruders continued, and that seemed strange to King. He could even hear their words: "I tell you it is he," said one voice; and another cried, "Hey, you, wake up!" Then King opened his eyes to look upon twenty brass cuirasses upon twenty sturdy warriors in the uniform of Lodivarman.

"So you have come back!" exclaimed one of the warriors. "I did not think you were such a fool."

"Neither did I," said King.

"Where is the girl?" demanded the speaker. "Lodivarman will be glad to have you, but he would rather have the girl."

"He will never get her," said King. "She is safe in the palace of her father at Pnom Dhek."

"Then it will go so much the harder for you," said the warrior, "and I am sorry for you, for you are certainly a courageous man."

King shrugged. He looked about him for some avenue of escape, but he was entirely surrounded now and the odds were twenty to one against him. Slowly he arose to his feet. "Here I am," he said. "What are you going to do with me?"

"We are going to take you to Lodivarman," replied the warrior who had spoken first. Then they took his weapons from him and tied his wrists behind his back. They were not cruel nor unduly rough, for in the hearts of these men, themselves brave, was admiration for the courage of their prisoner.

"I'd like to know how you did it," said a warrior walking next to King.

"Did what?" demanded the American.

"How you got into the King's apartment unseen and got out again with the girl. Three men have died for it already, but Lodivarman is no nearer a solution of the puzzle than he was at first."

"Who died and why?" demanded King.

"The major-domo, for one," said the warrior.

"The major-domo did naught but obey the orders of Lodivarman," said King.

"You seem to know a lot about it," replied the warrior; "yet that is the very reason that he died. For once in his life he should have disobeyed the King, but he failed to do so, and Lodivarman lay bound and gagged until Vay Thon came to his rescue."

"Who else died?" asked King.

"The sentry who was posted at the banquet door with you. He had to admit that he had deserted his post, leaving you there alone; and with him was slain the officer of the guard who posted you, a stranger inside the King's palace."

"And these were all?" asked King.

"Yes," said the warrior. And when King smiled he asked him why he smiled.

"Oh, nothing of any importance," replied the American. "I was just thinking." He was thinking that the guiltiest of all had escaped—the sentry who had permitted Fou-tan to beguile him into allowing them to pass out of the palace into the garden. He guessed that this man would not be glad to see him return.

"So even now Lodivarman does not know how I escaped from the palace?" he demanded.

"No, but he will," replied the man with a sinister grin.

"What do you mean?" asked the American.

"I mean that before he kills you he will torture the truth from you."

"Evidently my stay in Lodidhapura is to be a pleasant one," he said.

"I do not know how pleasant it will be," replied the warrior; "but it will be short."

"Perhaps I shall be glad of that," said King.

"It will be short, man, but it will seem an eternity. I have seen men die before to satisfy Lodivarman's wrath."

From his captors King learned that his discovery had been purely accidental; the party that had stumbled upon him constituted a patrol, making its daily rounds through the jungle in the vicinity of Lodidhapura. And soon the great city itself arose before King's eyes, magnificent in its ancient glory, but hard as the stone that formed its temples and its towers, and hard as the savage hearts that beat behind its walls. Into its building had gone the sweat and the blood and the lives of a million slaves; behind its frowning walls had been enacted two thousand years of cruelties and bloody crimes committed in the names of kings and gods.

"The mills of the gods!" soliloquised King. "It is not so remarkable that they grind exceedingly fine as it is that their masters can reach out of the ages across a world and lay hold upon a victim who scarce ever heard of them."

They were rapidly approaching one of the gates of Lodidhapura, at the portals of which King knew he must definitely abandon hope; and all that King found to excite his interest was his own apathy to his impending fate. He knew that his mind should be dwelling upon thoughts of escape, and yet he found himself assuming a fatalistic attitude of mind that could contemplate impending death with utmost composure, for, indeed, what had life to offer him? The orbit of his existence was determined by that shining sun about which his love revolved—his little flaming princess. Denied for ever the warmth and light of her near presence, he was a lost satellite, wandering aimlessly in the outer darkness and the cold of interstellar space. What had such an existence to offer against the peaceful oblivion of death?

Yet whatever his thoughts may have been there was no reflection of them in his demeanour, as with firm stride and high-held head he entered once again the city of Lodidha-pura, where immediately he and his escort were surrounded by curious crowds as word travelled quickly from mouth to mouth that the abductor of the dancing girl of the Leper King had been captured.

They took him to the dungeons beneath the palace of Lo-divarman, and there they chained him to a wall. As if he had been a wild beast they chained him with double chains, and the food that they brought was thrown upon the floor before him—food that one would have hesitated to cast before a beast. The darkness of his cell was mitigated by a window near the low-ceiling—an aperture so small that it might scarcely be dignified by the name of window, since nothing larger than a good-sized cat could have passed through it; yet it served its purpose in a meagre way by admitting light and air.

Once again, as it had many times in the past, a conviction sought foothold in King's mind that he was still the victim of the hallucinations of fever, for notwithstanding all his experiences since he had entered the jungle it did not seem possible that in this twentieth century he, a free-born American, could be the prisoner of a Khmer king. The idea was fantastic, preposterous, unthinkable. He resorted to all the time-worn expedients for proving the fallacy of mental aberration, but in the end he always found himself double-chained to a stone wall in a dark-foul-stinking dungeon.

Night came and with it those most hideous of nocturnal dungeon dwellers—the rats. He fought them off, but always they returned; and all night he battled with them until, when daylight came and they left him, he sank exhausted to the stone flagging of his cell.

Perhaps he slept then, but he could scarcely know, for it seemed that almost instantly a hand was laid upon his shoulder and he was shaken to wakefulness. It was the hand of Vama, the commander of the ten who first had captured him in the jungle; and so it was neither a rough nor unfriendly hand, for the brass-bound warrior could find in his heart only admiration for this courageous stranger who had dared to thwart the desires of the Leper King, whom he feared more than he respected.

"I am glad to see you again, Gordon King," said Vama, "but I am sorry that we meet under such circumstances. The rage of Lodivarman is boundless and from it no man may save you, but it may lessen the anguish of your last hours to know that you have many friends among the warriors of Lodidhapura."

"Thank you, Vama," replied King. "I have found more than friendship in the land of the Khmers, and if I also find death here, it is because of my own choosing. I am content with whatever fate awaits me, but I want you to know that your assurances of friendship will ameliorate whatever pangs of suffering death may hold for me. But why are you here? Has Lodivarman sent you to execute his sentence upon me?"

"He will not finish you so easily as that," replied Vama. "What he has in his mind I do not know. I have been sent to conduct you to his presence, a signal honour for you, attesting the impression that your act made upon him."

"Perhaps he wants to question me," suggested King.

"Doubtless," replied Vama, "but that he could have delegated to his torturers, who well know how to elicit whatever they wish from the lips of their victims."

Vama bent and unlocked the padlock that fettered King to the wall and led him into the corridor upon which his cell opened, where the rest of Vama's ten awaited to escort the prisoner into the presence of Lodivarman. Kau and Tchek were there with the others with whom King had become familiar while he served as a warrior of the royal guard of Lodivarman, Leper King of Lodidhapura. Rough were the greetings that they exchanged, but none the less cordial; and so, guarded by his own friends, Gordon King was conducted toward the audience chamber of Lodivarman.

14

My Lord the Tiger

Lodivarman, a malignant scowl upon his face, crouched upon his great throne. Surrounding him were his warlords and his ministers, his high priests and the officers of his household; and at his left knelt a slave bearing a great golden platter piled high with mushrooms. But for the moment Lodivarman was too intent upon his vengeance to be distracted even by the cravings of his unnatural appetite, for here at last he had within his grasp the creature that had centred upon itself all the unbridled rage of a tyrant.

Trembling with the anger that he could not conceal, Lodivarman glared at Gordon King as the prisoner was led to the foot of the dais below his throne.

"Where is the girl?" demanded the King angrily.

"The Princess Fou-tan is safe in the palace of Beng Kher," replied King.

"How did you get her away? Some one must have helped you. If you would save yourself the anguish of torture, speak the truth," cried Lodivarman, his voice trembling with rage.

"Lodivarman, the King, knows better than any other how I took Fou-tan from him," replied the American.

"I do not mean that," screamed Lodivarman, trembling. "Siva will see that you suffer sufficient agonies for the indignity that you put upon me, but I can curtail that if you will reveal your accomplices."

"I had no accomplices," replied King. "I took the Princess and walked out of your palace and no one saw me."

"How did you get out?" demanded Lodivarman.

King smiled. "You are going to torture me, Lodivarman,

and you are going to kill me. Why should I give you even the gratification of satisfying your curiosity? Wantonly you have already destroyed three men in your anger. I shall be the fourth. The life of any one of us is worth more than yours. If I could I would not add further to the debt that you must pay in the final accounting when you face God beyond the grave.''

''What do you know, stranger, of the gods of the Khmers?'' demanded Lodivarman.

''I know little or nothing of Brahma, of Vishnu, or Siva,'' replied King, ''but I do know that above all there is a God that kings and tyrants must face; and in His eyes even a good king is not greater than a good slave, and of all creatures a tyrant is the most despicable.''

''You would question the power of Brahma, of Vishnu, and of Siva!'' hissed Lodivarman. ''You dare to set your God above them! Before you die then, by the gods, you shall seek their mercy in your anguish.''

''Whatever my suffering may be, you will be its author, Lodivarman,'' replied King. ''The gods will have nothing to do with it.''

A minor priest came near and whispered in the King's ear. Vay Thon, the high priest, was there, too. The old man stood with his eyes fixed compassionately upon King, but he knew he was powerless to aid his friend, for who should know better than a high priest the power of kings and the futility of gods.

The priest appeared to be urging something upon his ruler with considerable enthusiasm.

Lodivarman listened to the whispered words of counsel, and then for some time he sat in thought. Presently he raised his eyes to King again. ''It pleases us to prove the power of our Gods, revealing their omnipotence to the eyes of our people. My Lord the Tiger knows no god; you shall contend with him. If your God be so powerful let him preserve you from the beast.'' Lodivarman helped himself to mushrooms and sank back in his throne. ''Take him to the pit of My Lord the Tiger," he said presently; "but do not liberate the great beast until we come."

The soldiers surrounded King and led him away, but before they had reached the doorway leading from the audience chamber Lodivarman halted them. "Wait!" he cried. "It shall not be said the Lodivarman is unfair even to an enemy. When this man enters the pit with My Lord the Tiger, see that he has a javelin wherewith to defend himself. I have heard stories of his prowess; let us see if they were exaggerated."

From the palace, King was led across the royal garden to the great temple of Siva; and there, upon one of the lower levels, a place where he had never been before, he was conducted to a small amphitheatre, in the centre of which was sunk a deep pit that was, perhaps, a hundred feet square. The entrance to the pit was down a stairway and along a narrow corridor of stone to massive wooden doors which the soldiers threw open.

"Enter, Gordon King," said Vama. "Here is my javelin, and may your God and my gods be with you."

"Thanks!" said King. "I imagine that I shall need them all," and then he stepped into the sunlit pit as the doors were closed behind him.

The floor and walls of the cubicle were of blocks of stone set without mortar, but so perfectly fitted that the joints were scarcely discernible. As King stood with his back against the doorway through which he had entered the pit, he saw in the wall opposite him another door of great planks, a low sinister door, behind which he guessed paced a savage, hungry carnivore.

King hefted the javelin in his hand. It was a sturdy, well-balanced weapon. Once again he recalled his college days when he had hurled a similar weapon beneath the admiring eyes of his mates; but then only distance had counted, only the superficial show that is the keynote of civilisation had mattered.

What mattered it that other men might cast a javelin more accurately? Which after all would be the practical test of efficiency. Gordon King could cast it farther than any of them, which was a feat far more showy than accuracy; but from the unlettered Che he had learned what college had failed to teach him and had acquired an accuracy as uncanny as the great distances that had won him fame.

Twice already had he met My Lord the Tiger and vanquished him with his javelin. Each time it had seemed to King a miracle. That it could be repeated again, that for the third time he could overcome the lord of Asia seemed incredible. And what would it profit him were he to succeed? From the cruel fangs and talons of the tiger he would be transferred to the greater cruelties of Lodivarman.

As he stood there upon the stone flagging of the pit beneath the hot sun that poured its unobstructed rays into the enclosure, he saw the audience sauntering to the stone benches that encircled the arena. It was evident that those who were to witness his destruction were members of the household of the King; princes and nobles and warriors there were and ministers and priests, and with them were their women. Last of all came Lodivarman with his bodyguard and slaves. To a canopied throne he made his way while the audience knelt, the meeker of them touching their foreheads to the stone flagging of the aisles. Before his throne Lodivarman halted, while his dead eyes swept quickly over the assembly, passing from them to the arena and the solitary warrior standing there below him. For a long moment the gaze of the King was riveted upon the American; hatred and suppressed rage were in that long, venomous appraisal of the man who had thwarted and humiliated him—that low creature that had dared lay profaning hands upon the person of the King.

Slowly Lodivarman sank into his throne. Then he made a brief sign to an attendant, and an instant later the notes of a trumpet floated out across the still air of the arena. The kneeling men and women arose and took their seats. Once again Lodivarman raised his hand, and again the trumpet sounded, and every eye was turned upon the low doorway upon the opposite side of the arena from the American.

King saw the heavy barrier rise slowly. In the darkness

beyond it nothing was visible at first, but presently he was aware that something moved within, and then he saw the familiar yellow and black stripes that he had expected. Slowly a great tiger stepped into the doorway, pausing upon the threshold, blinking from the glare of the sunlight. His attention was attracted first by the people upon the stone benches above him, and he looked up at them and growled. Then he looked down and saw King. Instantly his whole attitude changed. He half crouched, and his tail moved in sinuous undulations; his head was flattened, and his eyes glared fiercely.

Gordon King did not wait for the attack. He had a theory of his own based upon his experience with wild beasts. He knew them to be nervous and oftentimes timid when confronted by emergencies that offered aspects that were new and unfamiliar.

A gasp of astonishment, not unmingled with admiration, arose from the people lining the edges of the pit, for the thing that they witnessed was as surprising to them as King hoped it would be to the tiger—instead of the beast charging the man, they saw the man charging the beast. Straight toward the crouching carnivore King ran, his spear balanced and ready in his hand.

For an instant the tiger hesitated. He had expected nothing like this; and then he did what King had hoped that he might do, what he had known there was a fair chance that he would do. Fearful of the new and unexpected, the beast turned and broke, and as he did so he exposed his left side fully and at close range to the quick eye of his antagonist.

Swift as lightning moved King's spear-arm. The heavy javelin, cast with unerring precision and backed to the last ounce by the strength and the weight of the American, tore into the striped side just behind the left shoulder of the great beast. At the instant that the weapon left his hand King turned and raced to the far extremity of the arena. The running tiger, carried by his own momentum, rolled over and over upon the stone flagging; his horrid screams and coughing roars shook the amphitheatre. King was positive that the beast's heart was pierced, but he knew that these great cats were so tenacious of life that in the brief instant of their dying they often destroyed their adversaries also. It was for this reason that he had put as much distance as he could between himself and the infuriated animal, and it was well that he had done so, for the instant that the tiger had regained his feet he discovered King and charged straight for him.

Unarmed and helpless, the man stood waiting. Breathless, the spectators had arisen from their stone benches and were bending eagerly forward in tense anticipation of the cruel and bloody end.

Half the length of the arena the tiger crossed in great bounds. A sudden conviction swept the man that after all he had missed the heart. He was poised for what he already knew must be a futile leap to one side in an effort to dodge the first charge of the onrushing beast, when suddenly the tiger collapsed, seemingly in mid-air; and his great carcase came rolling across the flagging to stop at King's feet.

For an instant there was utter silence, and then a great shout rose from the spectators. "He has won his life, Lodivarman! He has won his freedom!" arose here and there from the braver among them, and the others cheered in approval.

Lodivarman, crouching in his throne with an ugly sneer upon his lips, called a functionary to him for a few, brief whispered instructions, and then the Leper King arose and passed through the kneeling people as he departed from the amphitheatre.

A moment later the door that had opened to admit King to the pit creaked again upon its hinges to admit Vama and an escort of warriors.

King greeted his former comrade with a smile. "Have you come to finish the work that the tiger failed to do," he asked, "or have you come to escort me to freedom?"

"Neither," replied Vama. "We have come to return you to your cell, for such are the commands of the King. But if he does not set you free eventually," added Vama in low tones, "it will be to the lasting disgrace of Lodivarman, for never was a man more deserving of his life and liberty than you. You are the first man, Gordon King, who has ever faced the tiger in this pit and come out alive.''

''Which does not at all satisfy Lodivarman's craving for revenge,'' suggested the American.

''I am afraid you are right,'' said Vama, as they moved along the corridor toward the dungeon, ''but you must know that to-day you have made many new friends in Lodidhapura, for there are those among us who can appreciate courage, strength and skill.''

''My mistake,'' said King, ''was not in my selection of friends, but in my selection of an enemy; for the latter, I have found one from whom all the friends in the world may not save me.''

Once again in his gloomy, cheerless cell King was fettered to the cold, familiar stone; but he was cheered by the kind words of Vama and the friendly expressions of other members of the guard that had escorted him hither; and when presently a slave came with food he, too, had words of praise and friendliness; and the food that he brought was well prepared and plentiful.

The day passed and the long night followed, and toward the middle of the next forenoon a visitor came to King's cell; and as he paused in the doorway, the prisoner recognised the yellow robe and the white beard of Vay Thon, the high priest of Siva, and his face lighted with pleasure, as the old man peered into the dim interior of his prison.

''Welcome, Vay Thon!'' he exclaimed, ''and accept my apologies for the mean hospitality that I may offer so distinguished and so welcome a guest.''

''Give that no thought, my son,'' replied the old man. ''It is enough that so courageous a warrior should receive a poor old priest with such pleasure as is evidenced by your tone. I am glad to be with you, but I wish that it might be under happier circumstances and that I might be the bearer of more welcome news.''

''You have brought news to me, then?'' asked King.

''Yes,'' replied Vay Thon. ''Because of what I owe you and for the friendship that I feel for you I have come to warn you, though any warning of your impending doom can avail you nothing."

"Lodivarman will not give me my liberty or my life, then?" asked King.

"No," replied Vay Thon. "The affront that you put upon him he considers beyond forgiveness. You are to be destroyed, but in such a way that the responsibility shall not rest upon the shoulders of Lodivarman."

"And how is this to be accomplished?" asked the American.

"You are to be summoned to the audience chamber of Lodivarman to receive your freedom and then you are to be set upon and assassinated by members of his guard. The story is to be spread that you sought to take the life of Lodivarman, so that his soldiers were compelled to slay you."

"Vay Thon," said King, "perhaps the warning that you bring me may not save me from the fate that Lodivarman has ordained; but it has demonstrated your friendship; and my last hours, therefore, will be happier because you came. And now go, for if the knowledge that you have imparted prompts me to take advantage of some opportunity for revenge or escape, there must be no clue to suggest that you are in any way responsible."

"I appreciate your thoughtfulness, my friend," replied the old priest, "and as I can be of no service to you I shall leave you, but know that constantly I shall supplicate the gods to protect you." He came and placed his hands upon King's shoulders. "Good-bye, my son, my heart is heavy," and as the tears welled in his old eyes he turned and left the cell.

Vay Thon had been gone but a short time when King heard the sound of footsteps approaching, and with these were mingled the clank of armour and the rattling of accoutrements. Presently, when the men halted before the doorway of his cell, he saw that they were all strangers to him. The officer who commanded them entered the cell, greeting King pleasantly.

"I bring you good news," he said, as he stooped and unlocked the padlock and cast King's fetters from him.

"Any news would be good news here," replied the American.

"But this is the best of all news," said the officer. "Lodivarman has commanded that you be conducted to him that he may grant you your freedom in person."

"Splendid," said King, though he could scarcely repress a smile as he recalled the message that Vay Thon had brought him.

Back to the now familiar audience chamber of the King they conducted the prisoner, and once again he stood before the throne of Lodivarman. There were few in attendance upon the monarch, a fact which suggested that he had not cared to share the secret of his perfidy with more than was absolutely necessary. But few though they were, the inevitable slave was there, kneeling at Lodivarman's side with his platter of mushrooms; and it was the sight of these lowly fungi that instantly riveted the attention of the doomed man, for suddenly they had become more important than brassbound soldiers, than palace functionaries, than the King himself, for they had suggested to the American a possible means of salvation.

He knew that he must think and act quickly, for he had no means of knowing how soon the signal for his assassination would be given.

Surrounded by his guards, he crossed the audience chamber and halted before the throne of Lodivarman. He should have prostrated himself then, but he did not; instead he looked straight into the dead eyes of the tyrant.

"Lodivarman," he said, "listen to me for a moment before you give the signal that will put into execution the plan that you have conceived, for at this instant your own life and happiness hang in the balance."

"What do you mean?" demanded Lodivarman.

"You questioned the power of my God, Lodivarman," continued King, "but you saw me vanquish My Lord the Tiger in the face of the wrath of Siva, and now you know that I am aware of just what you planned for me here. How could I have vanquished the beast, or how could I have known your plans except through the intervention and the favour of my God?''

Lodivarman seemed ill at ease. His eyes shifted suspiciously from one man to another. "I have been betrayed," he said angrily.

"On the contrary," replied King, "you have been given such an opportunity as never could have come to you without me. Will you hear me before I am slain?"

"I do not know what you are talking about. I sent for you to free you; but speak on, I am listening."

"You are a leper," said King, and at the hideous word Lodivarman sprang to his feet, trembling with rage, his face livid, his dead eyes glaring.

"Death to him!" he cried. "No man may speak that accursed word to me and live."

At Lodivarman's words warriors sprang menacingly toward King. "Wait!" cried the American. "You have told me that you would listen. Wait until I have spoken, for what I have to say means more to you than life itself."

"Speak, then, but be quick," snapped Lodivarman.

"In the great country from which I come," continued King, "there are many brilliant physicians who have studied all of the diseases to which mankind is heir. I, too, am a physician, and under many of those men have I studied and particularly have I studied the disease of leprosy. Lodivarman, you believe this disease to be incurable; but I, the man whom you would destroy, can cure you."

King's voice, well modulated but clear and distinct, had carried his words to every man in the audience chamber, and the silence which followed this dramatic declaration was so profound that one might have said that no man even breathed. All felt the tenseness of the moment.

Lodivarman, who had sunk back into his throne after his wild outburst of anger, seemed almost to have collapsed. He was trembling visibly, his lower jaw dropped upon his chest. King knew that the man was impressed, that all within the audience chamber were impressed, and his knowledge of human nature told him that he had won, for he knew that

Lodivarman, king though he was, was only human and that he would grasp at even the most impalpable suggestion of hope that might be offered him in the extremity of his fear and loathing for the disease that claimed him.

Presently the tyrant found his voice. "You can cure me?" he asked, almost piteously.

"My life shall be the forfeit," replied King, "on condition that you swear before your gods in the presence of Vay Thon, the high priest, that in return for your health you will grant me life and liberty—"

"Life, liberty, and every honour that lies within my power shall be conferred upon you," cried Lodivarman, his voice trembling with emotion. "If you rid me of this horrid sickness, aught that you ask shall be granted. Come, let us not delay. Cure me at once."

"The sickness has held you for many years, Lodivarman," replied King, "and it cannot be cured in a day. I must prepare medicine, and you must carry out the instructions that I shall give you, for I can cure you only if you obey me implicitly."

"How do I know that you will not poison me?" demanded Lodivarman.

King thought for a moment. Here was an obstacle that he had not foreseen, and then suddenly a solution suggested itself. "I can satisfy you as to that, Lodivarman," he replied, "for when I prepare medicine for you I shall take some of it myself in your presence."

Lodivarman nodded. "That will safeguard me," he said, "and now what else?"

"Put me where Vay Thon, the high priest, can watch me always. You trust him, and he will see that no harm befalls you through me. He will help me to obtain the medicine that I require, and to-morrow I shall be ready to commence the treatment. But in the meantime your system must be prepared to permit the medicine to take effect, and in this I can do nothing without your co-operation."

"Speak!" said Lodivarman. "Whatever you suggest I shall do."

"Have every mushroom in Lodidhapura destroyed," said King. "Have your slave burn those that have been prepared, and determine never to taste another."

Lodivarman scowled angrily. "What have mushrooms to do with the cure?" he demanded. "They afford me the only pleasure that I have in life. This is naught but a trick to annoy and discomfort me."

"As you will," said King with a shrug. "I can cure you, but only if you obey my instructions. My medicines will have no effect if you continue to eat mushrooms. But it is up to you, Lodivarman. Do as you choose."

For a time the ruler sat tapping nervously upon the arm of his throne, and then suddenly and almost savagely he turned upon the kneeling slave at his side. "Throw out the accursed things," he cried. "Throw them out! Destroy them! Burn them! And never let me set my eyes upon you again."

Trembling, the slave departed, carrying the platter of mushrooms with him, and then Lodivarman directed his attention upon one of the officers of his household. "Destroy the royal mushroom bed," he cried, "and see to it that you do it thoroughly," and then to another, "Summon Vay Thon." As the officers left the room Lodivarman turned to King again. "How long will it be before I am cured?" he asked.

"I cannot tell that until I see how you react to my medicine," replied the American; "but I believe that you will see almost immediate improvement. It may be very slow, and on the other hand, it may come very rapidly."

While they waited for Vay Thon, Lodivarman plied King with question after question; and now that he was convinced that men had been cured of leprosy and that he himself might be cured, a great change seemed to come over him. It was as though a new man had been born; his whole aspect appeared to change, as the hideous burden of fear and hopelessness that he had carried for so many years was dissipated by the authoritative manner and confident pronouncement of the American. And when Vay Thon entered the audience chamber, he saw a smile upon Lodivarman's face for the first time in so many years that he had almost forgotten that the man could smile.

Quickly Lodivarman explained the situation to Vay Thon and gave him his instructions relative to the American, for he wished the latter to hasten the preparation of his medicine.

"To-morrow," he cried, as the two men were backing from the apartment, "to-morrow my cure shall commence." And Gordon King did not tell him that his cure already had started, that it had started the instant that he had given orders for the destruction of the royal mushroom bed, for he did not wish Lodivarman to know what he knew—that the man was not a leper and never had been, that what in his ignorance he had thought was leprosy was nothing more than an aggravated form of dermatitis, resulting from food poisoning. At least King prayed that his diagnosis was correct.

15

War

From the quarters of Vay Thon slaves were despatched into the jungle for many strange herbs and roots, and from these King compounded three prescriptions, but the basis of each was a mild laxative. The purpose of the other ingredients was chiefly to add impressiveness and mystery to the compounds, for however much King might deplore this charlatanism he was keenly aware that he must not permit the cure to appear too simple. He was dealing with a primitive mind, and he was waging a battle of wits for his life—conditions which seemed to warrant the adoption of means that are not altogether frowned upon by the most ethical of modern practitioners.

Three times a day he went in person to a small audience chamber off the bedroom of Lodivarman, and there, in the presence of Vay Thon and officers of the royal household, he tasted the medicine himself before administering it to Lodivarman. Upon the third day it became apparent that the sores upon the body of the King were drying up. Exsiccation was so manifest that Lodivarman was jubilant. He laughed and joked with those about him and renewed his assurances to the American that no reward within the power of his giving would be denied him when Lodivarman was again a whole man. Each day thereafter the improvement was marked and rapid, until, at the end of three weeks, no trace remained of the hideous sores that had so horribly disfigured the monarch for so many years.

Gradually King had been diminishing the dosages that he had been administering and had tapered off the treatment from three to two a day and finally to one. Upon the twenty-first day King ordered Lodivarman to his bedroom; and there, in the presence of Vay Thon and three of the highest officers of the kingdom, he examined the King's entire body and found the skin clear, healthy, and without blemish.

"Well?" demanded Lodivarman, when the examination had been completed.

"Your Majesty is cured," said King.

The King arose from his bed and threw a robe about him. "Life and liberty are yours, Gordon King," he said. "A palace, slaves, riches are at your disposal. You have proven yourself a great warrior and a great physician. If you will remain here you shall be an officer in the royal guard and the private physician of Lodivarman, the King."

"There is but one reason why I care to remain in the land of the Khmers," replied King, "and that reason you must know, Lodivarman, before I can accept the honours that you would bestow upon me."

"And what is that?" demanded Lodivarman.

"To be as near as possible to the Princess Fou-tan of Pnom Dhek in the hope that some day I may claim her hand in marriage as already I have won her love."

"Already have I forgiven you for that act of yours which deprived me of the girl," said Lodivarman, without an instant's hesitation. "If you can win her, I shall place no obstacles in your path, but on the contrary I shall assist you in every way within my power. Let no man say that the gratitude of Lodivarman is tinged with selfishness or with revenge."

Lodivarman did even more than he had promised, for he created Gordon King a prince of Khmer, and so it was that the American found himself elevated from the position of the condemned criminal to that of the titled master of a palace—a lord over many slaves and the commander of five hundred Khmer warriors.

Great was the rejoicing in Lodidhapura when the King's cure became known; and for a week the city was given over to dancing, to pageants, and to celebration. In the howdah of the royal elephant at Lodivarman's side, King rode along the avenues of Lodidhapura in the van of a procession of a thousand elephants trapped in gorgeous silks and gold and jewels.

And then upon the last day, when the rejoicing was at its height, all was changed in the brief span of an instant. A sweat-streaked, exhausted messenger staggered to the gates of Lodidhapura; and ere he swooned from fatigue he gasped out his brief message to the captain of the gates.

"Beng Kher comes with a great army to avenge the insult to his Princess," and then he fell unconscious at the feet of the officer.

Quickly was the word carried to Lodivarman and quickly did it spread through the city of Lodidhapura. The gay trappings of a fête vanished like magic to be replaced by the grim trappings of war. Well worn and darkened with age were the housings and harnesses of the elephants as a thousand strong they filed from the north gates of Lodidhapura, bearing upon their backs the sturdy archers and spearmen of Lodivarman; and with them rode Gordon King, the prince, at the head of his new command. Alone upon a swift elephant he rode with only the mahout seated before him on the head of the great beast.

Little or nothing did the American know of the tactics of Khmer warfare, except that which he had derived from fellow warriors while he served among them and from other officers since his appointment. He had learned that the battles consisted principally of individual combat between elephant crews and that the duties of an officer did little more than constitute him a focal point upon which his men might rally for the pursuit if the enemy broke and retreated.

With long, rolling strides the elephants of war swung along the avenue into the jungle. Here and there were bits of colour or a glint of sunlight on a shining buckle, but for the most part the beasts were caparisoned with stern simplicity for the business of war. From the howdahs the burnished cuirasses of the warriors gave back the sunlight, and from the shaft of many a spear floated a coloured ribbon. The men themselves were grim and silent, or moved to coarse jokes and oaths as suited the individuality of each; and the music was from rough-throated trumpets and booming drums.

Toward a great clearing the army made its way and there awaited the coming of Beng Kher, for wars between Lodidhapura and Pnom Dhek were governed by age-old custom. Here for a thousand years their armies had met whenever Pnom Dhek attacked Lodidhapura. Here the first engagement must take place; and if the soldiers of Beng Kher could not pass the forces of Lodivarman, they must turn back in defeat. It was a game of war governed by strict rules up to the point where one side broke and fled. If the troops of Lodivarman broke here they would be pursued to the gates of Lodidhapura; and there, within the walls of the city, they would make their final stand. But if Beng Kher's troops broke first, Lodivarman could take credit for a victory and might pursue them or not as he chose. To elude one another by strategy, to attempt to gain the rear of an enemy were not to be countenanced, largely so, perhaps, from the fact that flanking and enveloping movements were impossible with elephant troops in a dense forest, where the only avenues of advance or retreat were the well-marked trails that were known to all.

The clearing, along the south side of which the troops of Lodivarman were drawn up, was some two miles in length by a half or three-quarters of a mile in width. The ground was slightly rolling and almost entirely denuded of vegetation, since it was in almost constant use for the training and drilling of elephant troops.

As the last of the great pachyderms wheeled into place, the drums and the trumpets were silent; and from out of the north, to the listening ears of the warriors, came faintly the booming of Pnom Dhek's war drums. The enemy was approaching. The men looked to arrows and bowstrings. The mahouts spoke soothingly and encouragingly to their mighty charges. The officers rode slowly up and down the line in front of their men, exhorting them to deeds of courage. As the sound of the enemy drums and trumpets drew nearer, the elephants became noticeably nervous. They swayed from side to side, raising and lowering their trunks and flapping their great ears.

In each howdah were many extra spears and great quantities of arrows. King, alone, had twenty spears in his howdah and fully a hundred arrows. When he had first seen them loaded upon his elephant it had not seemed possible that he was to use them against other men, and he had found himself rather shrinking from contemplation of the thought; but now with the sound of the war drums in his ears and the smell of leather and the stink of war elephants in his nostrils and with that long line of grim faces and burnished cuirasses at his back, he felt a sudden mad blood lust that thrilled him to the depths of his being. No longer was he the learned and cultured gentleman of the twentieth century, but as much a Khmer warrior as ever drew a bow for ancient Yacovarman, The King of Glory.

The enemy is coming. The blare of his trumpets resounds across the field of battle, and now the head of the enemy column emerges on to the field. The trumpets of Lodidhapura blare and her drums boom. An elephant lifts his trunk and trumpets shrilly. It is with difficulty now that the mahouts hold their charges in line.

The enemy line is finally formed upon the opposite side of the great field. For a moment drums and trumpets are stilled, and then a hoarse fanfare rolls across the clearing from the trumpeters of Beng Kher. "We are ready," it seems to say, and instantly it is answered from Lodivarman's side. Simultaneously now the two lines advance upon one another; and for a moment there is a semblance of order and discipline, but presently here and there an elephant forges ahead of his fellows. They break into a trot. King is almost run down by his own men.

"Forward!" he shouts to his mahout.

Pandemonium has broken loose. Trumpets and drums merge with the battle cries of ten thousand warriors. The elephants, goaded to anger, scream and trumpet in their rage. As the two lines converge, the bowmen loose a shower of arrows from either side; and now the curses and cries of wounded men and the shrill screaming of hurt elephants mingle with the trumpets and the bugles and the war cries in the mad diapason of war.

King found himself carried forward on the crest of battle straight toward a lone officer of the enemy forces. He was riding the swaying howdah now like a sailor on the deck of a storm-tossed ship. The antagonist approaching him was balancing his javelin, waiting until they should come within surer range; but King did not wait. He was master of his weapon, and he had no doubts. Behind him were his men. He did not know that they were watching him; but they were, for he was a new officer and this his first engagement. His standing with them would be determined now forever. All of them had heard of his prowess and many of them had doubted the truth of the stories they had heard. They saw his spear-arm come back, they saw the heavy weapon flying through the air and a hoarse cheer broke from their throats as the point crashed through the burnished cuirass of the enemy.

An instant later the two lines came together with such terrific force that a score of elephants were overthrown. King was almost pitched from his howdah; and an instant later he was fighting hand to hand, surrounded by the warriors of Beng Kher. The battle now resolved itself into a slow milling of elephants as the mahouts sought to gain advantageous positions for the crews in their howdahs. Here and there a young elephant, or one sorely wounded and driven mad by pain, broke from the mêlee and bolted for the jungle. Warriors leaped from their howdahs, risking injury rather than the almost certain death that would await them as the frightened beasts stampeded through the forest. Only the mahouts clung to their posts, facing death rather than the disgrace of abandoning their charges. The hot sun blazed down upon the stinking, sweating mass of war. The feet of the milling elephants raised clouds of dust through which it was sometimes difficult to see more than a few yards.

In the moment that King was surrounded an arrow grazed his arm, while a dozen glanced from his helmet and his cuirass. His impressions were confused. He saw savage, distorted faces before him, at which he lunged with a long javelin. He was choked with dust and blinded by sweat. He heard the savage trumpeting of his own elephant and the shouts and curses of his mahout. It seemed impossible that he could extricate himself from such a position, or that he could long survive the vicious attack that was being directed upon him by the men of the officer he had slain; and then some of his own elephants came charging in, and a moment later he was surrounded by the warriors of his own command.

Ever forward they pushed. What was happening elsewhere in the line they did not know, for obscuring dust hid all but those close to them. The line before them gave; and then it held and pushed them back again, and so the battle surged to and fro and back and forth. But always it seemed to King that his side gained a little more at each advance than it lost. Presently the enemy line gave way entirely. King saw the elephants of Pnom Dhek turn in the murky dust and race toward the north. Just what the rest of the line was doing he did not know; and for the moment none of his own men was visible, so thick and heavy hung the pall of dust upon the field of battle.

Perhaps King forgot what little of the rules of Khmer warfare he had ever learned. Perhaps he thought only of following up an advantage already gained; but be that as it may, he shouted to his men to follow and ordered his mahout to pursue the fleeing warriors to Pnom Dhek. Amid the din of battle his men did not hear him, and so it was that, alone, Gordon King pursued that part of the enemy line that had broken directly in front of him.

Presently, as they drew away from the centre of the field and the dust clouds became less impenetrable, King saw the grey bulk of an elephant moving just ahead of him; and then as the visibility increased he saw still other enemy elephants farther in advance. Now he could see that there were two men in the howdah of the elephant just in front of him; but as he raised his javelin to cast it, he suddenly recognised the

man at whom his weapon was to be directed—it was Beng
Kher, King of Pnom Dhek and father of Fou-tan. King lowered his spear-arm; he could not slay the father of the girl he
loved. But who was his companion? Through the lessening
dust King sensed a vague familiarity in that figure. It occurred to him that he might take Beng Kher prisoner and thus
force him to sanction his marriage with Fou-tan. Other mad
schemes passed through his head as the two swift elephants
raced across the clearing.

Neither Beng Kher nor his companion appeared to be paying any attention to the warrior pursuing them, which convinced King that they believed him to be one of their own
men. King saw Beng Kher's companion lean forward over
the front of the howdah as though issuing instructions to the
mahout; and almost immediately their course was changed
to the right, while ahead of them King saw the other elephants that had accompanied Beng Kher disappearing into
the forest to the north.

The air about them was comparatively free from dust now,
so that King could see all that transpired about him. He
glanced behind; and from the clouds of dust arising from the
centre of the field he knew that the battle was still raging,
but he kept on in pursuit of the King of Pnom Dhek.

To his dismay he saw that the royal elephant was drawing
away from him, being swifter than his own. He saw something else, too—he saw Beng Kher remonstrating with his
companion, and then for the first time he recognised the
other man in the howdah as Bharata Rahon.

King was exhorting his mahout to urge the elephant to
greater speed; and when he glanced up again at the two men
in the howdah ahead of him, he saw Bharata Rahon suddenly
raise a knife and plunge it into the neck of Beng Kher. The
King staggered backward; and before he could regain his
equilibrium Bharata Rahon leaped forward and gave him a
tremendous shove, and King saw Beng Kher, the ruler of
Pnom Dhek, topple backward out of the howdah and plunge
to the ground below.

Horrified by the ruthless crime he had witnessed and

moved by the thought of Fou-tan's love for her father, King ordered his mahout to bring their elephant to a stop; and then sliding quickly from the howdah, he ran to where Beng Kher lay. The King was half stunned and blood was gushing from the wound in his neck. As best he could and as quickly, King stanched the flow; but what was he to do? Beng Kher was indeed his prisoner, but what would it profit him now?

He signalled his mahout to bring the elephant closer and make it lie down, and then the two men lifted the wounded Beng Kher into the howdah.

"What do you want with a wounded enemy?" demanded the mahout, and it was evident to King that the fellow had not recognised Beng Kher as King of Pnom Dhek. "Why do you not kill him?" continued the man.

"You were detailed to drive my elephant and not to question my acts," snapped King shortly, and whatever thoughts concerning the matter the mahout had thereafter he kept to himself.

"Whither, my lord?" he asked presently.

That was the very question that was bothering King—whither! Were he to take Beng Kher back to Lodidhapura, he did not know but that Lodivarman might destroy him. If he tried to take him back to Pnom Dhek, Beng Kher might die before they reached the city, or if he lived, doubtless he would see that King died shortly thereafter. The American had no love for Beng Kher, but if he could protect Fou-tan from grief by saving the life of her father, he would do so if he could but find the means; and presently a possible solution of his problem occurred to him.

He turned to his mahout. "I wish to go to the jungle south of Lodidhapura, avoiding the city and all men upon the way. Do you understand?"

"Yes, my lord," replied the man.

"Then make haste. I must reach a certain spot before dark. When we have passed Lodidhapura I will give you further directions."

Little Uda was playing before the dwelling of Che and Kangrey when he heard a sound that was familiar to him—

the approach of an elephant along the jungle trail that passed not far from where he played. Now and then elephants passed that way and sometimes little Uda saw them, but more often he did not. Uda and Che and Kangrey had no fear of these passing elephants, for the massive stone ruin in which they lived was off the beaten trail among a jumble of fallen ruins that was little likely to tempt the feet of the great pachyderms; so little Uda played on, giving scant heed to the approaching footsteps, but presently his keen ears noted what his eyes could not see; and leaping to his feet, he ran quickly into the dwelling, where Kangrey was preparing food for the evening meal before the return of Che.

"Mamma," cried Uda, "an elephant is coming. He has left the trail and is coming here."

Kangrey stepped to the doorway. To her astonishment she saw an elephant coming straight toward her dwelling. She only saw his feet and legs at first; and then, as he emerged from behind a tree that had hidden the upper part of his body, the woman gave a cry of alarm, for she saw that the elephant was driven by a mahout and that there was a warrior in the howdah upon its back. Grasping Uda by the hand, she sprang from her dwelling, bent upon escaping from the feared power of Lodivarman; but a familiar voice halted her, calling her by name.

"Do not be afraid, Kangrey," came the reassuring voice. "It is I, Gordon King."

The woman stopped and turned back, a smile of welcome upon her face. "Thanks be to the gods that it is you, Gordon King, and not another," she exclaimed. "But what brings you thus upon a great elephant and in the livery of Lodivarman to the poor dwelling of Kangrey?"

The mahout had brought the elephant to a stop now before Kangrey's doorway, and at his command the great beast lowered its huge body to the ground.

"I have brought a wounded warrior to you, Kangrey," said King, "to be nursed back to life and health as once you nursed me," and with the help of the mahout he lifted Beng Kher from the howdah.

"For you, Gordon King, Kangrey would nurse Lodivarman himself," said the woman.

They carried Beng Kher into the dwelling and laid him upon a pallet of dry grasses and leaves covered with the pelts of wild animals. Together King and Kangrey removed the golden cuirass from the fallen monarch. Taking off the rough bandages with which the American had stanched the flow of blood and covered the wounds, the woman bathed the gashes with water brought by Uda. Her deft fingers worked lightly and quickly; and while she prepared new bandages she sent Uda into the jungle to fetch certain leaves, which she laid upon the wounds beneath the bandages.

The mahout had returned to his elephant; and as Kangrey and King were kneeling upon opposite sides of the wounded man, Beng Kher opened his eyes. For a moment they roved without comprehension about the interior of the rude dwelling and from the face of the woman leaning above him to that of the man, upon whom he noted the harness of Lodivarman, and King saw that Beng Kher did not recognise him.

"Where am I?" asked the wounded man. "What has happened? But I need not ask. I fell in battle and I am a prisoner in the hands of my enemy."

"No," replied King, "you are in the hands of friends, Beng Kher. This woman will nurse you back to health; after that we shall decide what is to be done."

"Who are you?" demanded Beng Kher, scrutinising the features of his captor.

From beneath his cuirass and his leather tunic the American withdrew a tiny ring that was suspended about his neck on a golden chain, and when Beng Kher saw it he voiced an exclamation of surprise.

"It is Fou-tan's," he said. "How came you by it, man?"

"Do you not recognise me?" demanded the American.

"By Siva, you are the strange warrior who dared aspire to the love of the Princess of Pnom Dhek. The gods have deserted me."

"Why do you say that?" demanded King. "I think they have been damn' good to you."

"They have delivered me into the hands of one who may profit most by destroying me," replied Beng Kher.

"On the contrary, they have been kind to you, for they have given you into the keeping of the man who loves your daughter. That love, Beng Kher, is your shield and your buckler. It has saved you from death, and it will see that you are brought back to health."

For a while the King of Pnom Dhek lay silent, lost in meditation, but presently he spoke again. "How came I to this sorry pass?" he asked. "We were well out of the battle, Bharata Rahon and I—by Siva, I remember now!" he exclaimed suddenly.

"I saw what happened, Beng Kher," said King. "I was pursuing you and was but a short distance behind when I saw Bharata Rahon suddenly stab you and then throw you from the howdah of your elephant."

Beng Kher nodded. "I remember it all now," he said. "The traitorous scoundrel! Fou-tan warned me against him, but I would not believe her. There were others who warned me, but I was stubborn. He thought he had killed me, eh? but he has not. I shall recover and have my revenge, but it will be too late to save Fou-tan."

"What do you mean?" demanded Gordon King.

"I can see his plan now as plainly as though he had told me in his own words," said Beng Kher. "By now he is on his way to Pnom Dhek. He will tell them that I fell in battle. He will force Fou-tan to marry him, and thus he will become King of Pnom Dhek. Ah, if I had but one of my own people here I could thwart him yet."

"I am here," said Gordon King, "and it means more to me to prevent Bharata Rahon from carrying out his design than it could to any other man." He rose to his feet.

"Where are you going?" demanded Beng Kher.

"I am going to Pnom Dhek," replied King, "and if I am not too late I shall save Fou-tan; and if I am, I shall make her a widow."

"Wait," said Beng Kher. He slipped a massive ring from one of his fingers and held it out to the American. "Take this," he said. "In Phom Dhek it will confer upon you the authority of Beng Kher, the King. Use it as you see fit to save Fou-tan and to bring Bharata Rahon to justice. Farewell, Gordon King, and may the gods protect you and give you strength."

Gordon King ran from the dwelling and leaped into the howdah of his elephant. "Back to Lodidhapura," he commanded the mahout, "and by the shortest route as fast as the beast can travel."

16

In the Palace of Beng Kher

Lodivarman, the King, was resting after the battle that had brought victory to his arms. Never had he been in a happier mood; never had the gods been so kind to him. Free from the clutches of the loathsome disease that had gripped him for so many years and now victorious over his ancient enemy, Lodivarman had good reason for rejoicing. Yet there was a shadow upon his happiness, for he had lost many brave soldiers and officers during the engagement, and not the least of these was the new prince, Gordon King, whom he looked upon not only as his saviour, but as his protector from disease in the future. At his orders many men had searched the battlefield for the body of his erstwhile enemy, whom he now considered his most cherished captain; but no trace of it had been found, nor of his elephant nor his mahout; and it was the consensus of opinion that the beast, frenzied by wounds and terrified by the din of conflict, had bolted into the forest and that both men had been killed as the elephant plunged beneath the branches of great trees. A hundred warriors still were searching through the jungle, but no word had come from them. There could be but slight hope that the new prince lived.

While Lodivarman lay upon his royal couch, grieving perhaps more for himself than for Gordon King, a palace functionary was announced. "Admit him," said Lodivarman.

The courtier entered the apartment and dropped to one knee. "What word bring you?" demanded the King.

"The prince, Gordon King, seeks audience with Lodivarman," announced the official.

"What?" demanded Lodivarman, raising himself to a sitting position upon the edge of his couch. "He lives? He has returned?"

"He is alive and unhurt, Your Majesty," replied the man.

"Fetch him at once," commanded Lodivarman, and a moment later Gordon King was ushered into his presence.

"The gods have been kind indeed," said Lodivarman. "We thought that you had fallen in battle."

"No," replied King. "I pursued the enemy too far into the jungle, but in doing so I discovered something that means more to me than my life, Lodivarman, and I have come to you to enlist your aid."

"You have but to ask and it shall be granted," replied the King.

"The prince, Bharata Rahon, of Pnom Dhek, assassinated Beng Kher and is now hastening back to Pnom Dhek to force the Princess, Fou-tan, to wed him; and I have hastened to you to ask for men and elephants wherewith I may pursue Bharata Rahon and save Fou-tan from his treachery."

Perhaps this was a bitter pill for Lodivarman to swallow, for no man, not even a king, may easily forget humiliation—perhaps a king least of all—and he did not like to be reminded that Fou-tan had spurned him and that this man had taken her from him. But more powerful than his chagrin was his sincere gratitude to Gordon King, and so it is only fair to record that he did not hesitate an instant when he had heard the American's request.

"You shall have everything that you require—warriors, elephants, everything. You have heard?" he demanded, turning to an official standing near him.

The man nodded. "It is the King's command, then," continued Lodivarman, "that the prince be furnished at once with all he requires."

"A hundred elephants and five hundred men will answer my purpose," said King, "the swiftest elephants and the bravest warriors."

"You shall have them," said Lodivarman.

"I thank Your Majesty," said King. "And now permit me

to depart, for if I am to be successful there is no time to lose.''

"Go," said Lodivarman, "and may the gods accompany you."

Within the hour a hundred elephants and five hundred warriors swung through the north gate of Lodidhapura along the broad avenue beyond and into the jungle.

Far to the north, hastening through the forest to Pnom Dhek, moved Beng Kher's defeated army; and in the van was the Prince, Bharata Rahon, gloating in anticipation over the fruits of his villainy. Already was he demanding and receiving the rights and prerogatives of royalty, for he had spread the word that Beng Kher had been killed in battle and that he was hastening to Pnom Dhek to wed the Princess Fou-tan.

Early in the forenoon of the second day following the battle, Fou-tan, from her palace window, saw the column of returning elephants and warriors emerge from the forest. That the trumpets and the drums were mute told her that defeat had fallen upon the forces of the King, her father, and there were tears in her eyes as she turned away from the window and threw herself upon her couch.

Perhaps an hour later one of her little ladies-in-waiting came to her. "The Prince, Bharata Rahon, awaits you in the audience chamber, my Princess," she said.

"Has not my father, the King, sent for me?" demanded Fou-tan.

"The Prince brings word from your father," replied the girl, and there was that in her tone more than in her words that sent a qualm of apprehension through the heart of the little Princess.

She arose quickly. "Send word to Bharata Rahon, the Prince, that the Princess comes," she said. Quickly her slaves attended to her toilet, removing the traces that the tears had left and replacing the loosened strands of her hair.

In the corridor outside of her apartment awaited the functionaries that would accompany her to the audience chamber and Indra Sen in command of a detachment of the warriors of her guard, for the little Princess Fou-tan moved only with pomp and ceremony.

Through her own private entrance she came into the audience chamber, where she saw congregated the high officers of Pnom Dhek, the priests of the temple, and the captains in their burnished cuirasses and helmets; and as she came they knelt until she had reached the foot of the empty throne, where Bharata Rahon stood to receive her.

"Where is the King, my father?" she asked in a frightened voice.

"Beloved Princess," replied Bharata Rahon, "I bring you sad news."

"The King is dead!" cried Fou-tan.

Bharata Rahon inclined his head in assent. "He fell in battle bravely," he said, "but before he died he entrusted to me his last command to you."

"Speak," said the girl.

"It is believed that Lodivarman will follow up his victory and attack Pnom Dhek, and in addition to this we are threatened by enemies within our own walls—conditions which require a king upon the throne; and so it was your father's dying command that you wed at once, that Pnom Dhek may be ruled and guided by a man through the dangers which confront her."

"And the man that I am to marry is you, of course," said Fou-tan coldly.

"Who other could it be, my Princess?" asked Bharata Rahon.

"This is a matter which I do not care to discuss in public audience," said Fou-tan. "After a suitable period of mourning for my father, the King, we may perhaps speak of the matter again."

Bharata Rahon quelled the anger that arose in his heart and spoke in soft tones. "I can well appreciate the feelings of Your Majesty at this time," he said, "but the matter is urgent. Please dismiss everyone and listen to me in patience for a moment."

"Send them away then," said Fou-tan wearily, and when

the audience chamber had been cleared, she nodded to Bharata Rahon. "Speak," she said, "but please be brief."

"Fou-tan," said the Prince, "I would that you would wed me willingly, but the time now has passed for all childishness. We must be wed to-night. It is imperative. I can be King without you, for I have the men and the power. But there are others who would rally around you, and Pnom Dhek would be so weakened by civil war that it would fall an easy prey to Lodivarman. To-night in this hall the high priest shall wed us, if it is necessary to drag you here by force."

"It will be by force then," said Fou-tan, and, rising, she called to her guard that stood waiting just beyond the doorway.

"By force then," snapped Bharata Rahon, "and you will see how easily it may be done." As he spoke he pointed to the guardsmen entering the audience chamber to escort Foutan to her quarters.

"These are not my men," she cried. "Where is Indra Sen? Where are the warriors of my guard?"

"They have been dismissed, Fou-tan," replied Bharata Rahon. "The future King of Pnom Dhek will guard his Queen with his own men."

The Princess Fou-tan made no reply as, surrounded by the soldiers of Bharata Rahon, she left the audience chamber and returned to her own apartment, where a new surprise and indignity awaited her. Her slaves and even her ladies-in-waiting had been replaced by women from the palace of Bharata Rahon.

Her case seemed hopeless. Even the high priest, to whom in her extremity she might have turned for succour, would be deaf to her appeal, for he was bound by ties of blood to the house of Bharata Rahon and would be the willing and eager tool of his kinsman.

"There is only one," she murmured to herself, "and he is far away. Perhaps, even, he is dead. Would that I, too, were dead." And then she recalled what Bharata Rahon had said of the great danger that menaced Pnom Dhek, and her breast was torn by conflicting fears, which were lighted by no faintest ray of hope or happiness.

All during the long hours that followed, Fou-tan sought for some plan of escape from her predicament; but at every turn she was thwarted, for when she sought to send a message to Indra Sen, summoning him to her, and to other officials of the palace and the state whom she knew to be friendly to her, she found she was virtually a prisoner and that no message could be delivered by her except through Bharata Rahon, nor could she leave her apartment without his permission.

She might have melted into tears in her grief and anger, but the Princess of Pnom Dhek was made of sterner stuff. Through the long hours she sat in silence while slaves prepared her for the nuptial ceremony; and when at last the hour arrived, it was no little weeping queen that was escorted through the corridors of the palace toward the great audience chamber where the ceremony was to be performed, but a resentful, angry little queen with steel in her heart and another bit of shining, sharpened steel hidden in the folds of her wedding gown; and on her lips was a whispered plea to Siva, the Destroyer, to give her the strength to plunge the slim blade into the heart of Bharata Rahon or into her own before morning dawned again.

Through the dark forest from the south moved a hundred elephants, their howdahs filled with grim, half-savage warriors. At their head rode Gordon King chafing at the slow pace which the darkness and the dangers of the jungle imposed upon them.

Riding the howdah with King was an officer who knew well the country around Pnom Dhek and he it was who directed the mahout through the night. Presently he caused the elephant to be halted.

"We are nearing Pnom Dhek now," he said, "and are very close to the point upon the trail which you described to me."

"Bring the torch then and come with me," said King, and

together the two men descended to the ground where the officer lighted the flare and handed it to King.

Moving slowly along the trail, the American carefully examined the trees at his left, and within a hundred yards of the point at which they had left the column he halted.

"Here it is," he said. "Go and fetch the warriors, dismounted. Direct the mahouts to hold the elephants here until we return or until they receive further orders from me. Make haste. I shall await you here."

In the great assembly hall of the palace of Beng Kher were gathered the nobles of Pnom Dhek. The captains and the priests were there in glittering armour and gorgeous vestments, their women resplendent in silks and scintillating gems. Upon a raised dais the Prince Bharata Rahon and the Princess Fou-tan were seated upon thrones. The high priest of Siva stood between them, while massed in a half-circle behind them stood the nobles of the house of Bharata Rahon and the glittering warriors, who were their retainers. Among these was none of Fou-tan's allies. Neither Indra Sen nor any other officer or man of her personal guard was in the audience chamber, nor had she seen or heard aught of these since she had been conducted to the audience chamber in the morning. She wondered what fate had befallen them, and her heart was filled with fear for their safety, realising as well she might the extremes to which Bharata Rahon might go in his ruthless greed for power.

Before the dais the apsarases were dancing to drum and xylophone, cymbal and flute. The little dancers, nude above the waist, stepped and postured through the long ritual of the sacred dance; but Fou-tan, though her eyes stared down upon them, did not see them. All that she saw was the figure of a warrior in battered brass—a warrior with bronzed skin and clear eyes, who had held her in his arms and spoken words of love into her ear. Where was he? He had told Indra Sen that he would never leave the jungle, that always he would be near; and Indra Sen had repeated his words to Fou-tan— words that she had cherished in her heart above all the jewels of memory. How close he seemed to-night! Never since he had departed had Fou-tan so felt his presence hovering near, nor ever had she so needed him. With a quick, short sigh that was half a gasp she shook herself into a realisation of the futility of her dreams. Now she saw the apsarases. Their dance was drawing to a close. When it was over the high priest and his acolytes would initiate the ceremony that would make Fou-tan the wife of Bharata Rahon and give Pnom Dhek a new king.

As the girl shuddered at the thought and her fingers closed upon the hilt of the dagger beneath her gorgeous robe, a man stumbled through the darkness of the night toward the outer walls of Pnom Dhek; and behind him, silent as spectres from another world, came five hundred brass-bound men-at-arms.

No light guided them now, for they were approaching the guarded walls of the city; but so indelibly fixed in the memory of Gordon King was this way which he had traversed but once before that he needed no light. Into the mouth of a shallow ravine he led his warriors; and toward its head, where the wall of Pnom Dhek crossed it, he found a little doorway, well hidden by shrubbery and vines. So well hidden was this secret passage, planned by some long dead king, that no bar secured the door that closed its entrance—a precaution made necessary, doubtless to satisfy the requirements of a king who might find it necessary to enter as well as to leave the city in haste and secrecy. But whatever the reason it was a godsend this night to Gordon King as he led his spearmen and his archers beneath the city of Pnom Dhek toward the palace of Beng Kher.

Once safely within the corridor, they lighted their torches; and in the flickering, smoky flame the column moved noiselessly toward its destination. They had gone a considerable distance passing the openings to other corridors and to dark chambers that flanked their line of march, when Gordon King was confronted by the disheartening realisation that he had lost his way. He knew that when Indra Sen and Hamar had led him from the palace they had not passed through any corridor resembling that in which he now found himself. For the moment his heart sank, and his high hopes waned.

To be lost in this labyrinthine maze beneath the palace and the city was not only discouraging but might well prove fatal to his plan and, perhaps, to the safety and the lives of his command. He felt that he must keep the truth from his followers as long as possible, lest the effect upon their morale might prove disastrous; and so he moved boldly on, trusting that chance would guide him to a stairway leading to the level of the ground above.

His mind was harassed by unhappy apprehensions concerning Fou-tan. He was obsessed by the conviction that she was in dire and imminent peril, and the thought left him frantic because of his helplessness.

Such was his state of mind when, as he was passing along a corridor flanked on either side by dark and gloomy doorways, he saw that the passageway he was following ended at a transverse corridor. Which way should he turn? He knew that he could not hesitate, and at that moment he heard a voice calling his name from the interior of a dark cell beyond one of the gloomy doorways.

King halted as did the men near him, startled and apprehensive, their weapons ready. King stepped toward the doorway from which the voice had come.

"Who speaks?" he demanded.

"It is I—Indra Sen," replied the voice, and with a sigh of relief that was almost a gasp King stepped quickly to the low doorway.

The light of his torch illuminated a narrow cell, upon the floor of which squatted Indra Sen, chained to the wall.

"May the gods be thanked that you have come, Gordon King," cried the young Khmer officer; "and may they grant that you are not too late to prevent a tragedy."

"What do you mean?" demanded King.

"Fou-tan is to be forced to wed Bharata Rahon tonight," replied Indra Sen. "Perhaps the ceremony already has been performed. All those whose duty it is to defend Fou-tan have been chained in the dungeon here."

"Where is the ceremony to be performed?" demanded King.

"In the great audience chamber," replied Indra Sen.

"Can you lead me there by the shortest route?"

"Take off my fetters and those of my men and I will not only lead you, but we will strike with you in the service of our Princess."

"Good!" exclaimed Gordon King. "Where are your men?"

"Along both sides of this corridor."

To release them all was the work of but a few moments, for willing hands and strong struck off the fetters; and then, directed by Indra Sen, the party moved quickly on to its work. The warriors of Fou-tan's guard had no weapons other than their bare hands and the hatred that was in their hearts, but once within the audience chamber they knew that they would find weapons upon the bodies of their antagonists.

The high priest of Siva stepped forward and, turning, faced Bharata Rahon and Fou-tan. "Arise," he said, "and kneel."

Bharata Rahon stepped from his throne half-turning to await Fou-tan, but the girl sat rigid on her carved chair.

"Come," whispered Bharata Rahon.

"I cannot," said Fou-tan, addressing the high priest.

"You must, my Princess," urged the priest.

"I loathe him. I cannot mate with him."

Bharata Rahon stepped quickly toward her. His lips were smiling for the benefit of those who watched from below the dais; but in his heart was rage, and cruel was the grip that he laid upon the gentle wrist of Fou-tan.

"Come," he hissed, "or by the gods you shall be slain, and I shall rule alone."

"Then slay me," said Fou-tan. But he dragged her to her feet; and those below saw his smiling face and thought that he was merely assisting the little Princess, who had been momentarily overcome by the excitement of the occasion.

And then a great hanging parted at the rear of the dais behind the throne, and a warrior stepped out behind the semi-circle of those that half-surrounded Bharata Rahon and his unwilling bride. Perhaps some in the audience saw the tall warrior; perhaps at the instant they were moved to surprise, but before they could give an alarm, or before they could realise that an alarm was necessary, he had shouldered his way roughly through the cordon of warriors standing between him and the three principals at the front of the dais, and behind him the doorway through which he had come spewed a torrent of hostile warriors.

Cries of alarm arose simultaneously from the audience and from the warriors of Bharata Rahon who stood upon the dais, and above all in sudden fury burst the war-cry of Lodidhapura.

Simultaneously Bharata Rahon and Fou-tan wheeled about and instantly recognised Gordon King, but with what opposite emotions!

With a curse Bharata Rahon drew his sword. A dozen spearmen leaped toward the rash intruder only to be hurled back by the warriors of Lodidhapura and the unarmed soldiers of Fou-tan's guard, led by Indra Sen.

"Dog of a slave!" cried Bharata Rahon, as the two men stood face to face, and at the same time he swung a heavy blow at King's helmet—a blow that King parried and returned so swiftly that the Khmer prince had no defence ready.

It was a fearful blow that Gordon King struck, for love of a princess and to avenge a king. Down through the golden helmet of the false prince his blade clove into the brain of Bharata Rahon; and as the body lunged forward upon the dais, King swung around to face whatever other antagonist might menace him. But he found himself entirely surrounded by his own warriors, and a quick glance about the audience chamber showed him that his orders had been followed to the letter. So quickly had they moved that at every entrance now stood a company of his brass-bound soldiers.

There had been little resistance, for so sudden had been the attack and so overwhelming the surprise of the men of Pnom Dhek that those in the audience chamber had been completely surrounded by a superior force before many of them had realised what was happening.

Indra Sen and his warriors had succeeded in wresting weapons from the men of Bharata Rahon, and with them

King now dominated the situation, at least in the audience chamber; though in the city without were thousands of warriors who might easily overcome them. But this King had foreseen and had no intention of permitting.

Turning toward the surprised men and women in the audience chamber, he raised his hand. "Silence!" he cried. "Let no man raise a weapon against us, and none shall be harmed. I came here not to attack Pnom Dhek but to avenge her King. Beng Kher did not fall in battle; he was stabbed by Bharata Rahon. He is not dead. Beng Kher is still King of Pnom Dhek."

A cheer arose from Indra Sen and his warriors, in which joined many in the audience chamber, for with Bharata Rahon dead they no longer feared him and quickly returned their allegiance to their King.

Fou-tan came close to the tall warrior standing there beside the body of Bharata Rahon and facing the officers and the dignitaries of the court of Beng Kher. She touched him gently. "My Gordon King!" she whispered. "I knew that you were near. I knew that you would come. But tell me again that my father is not dead and that he is safe."

"He is wounded, Fou-tan; but I have left him with honest people who will nurse him, the same who nursed me when I was lost and ill in the jungle. He sent me here to save you from Bharata Rahon, though I would have come without the sending. Here is the priest, Fou-tan, and you are in your wedding-gown. Is it in your heart to deny me again?"

"What would my father say?" she murmured, hesitatingly, and then suddenly she raised her head proudly. "He is not here, and I am Queen!" she exclaimed. "I care not what any man may say. If you will have me, Gordon King, I am yours!"

King turned toward the audience. "The scene is set for a wedding," he said in clear tones. "The priest is here; the bride is ready. Let the ceremony proceed."

"But the groom is dead!" cried one of Bharata Rahon's lieutenants.

"I am the groom," said King.

"Never!" cried another voice. "You are naught but a Lodidhapurian slave."

"He is neither slave nor Lodidhapurian," said Fou-tan. "He is the man of my choice, and to-night I am Queen."

"Never! Never!" shouted many voices.

"Listen!" exclaimed the American. "It is not within your power to dictate, for to-night the Princess Fou-tan is Queen; and I am your conqueror."

"You are already surrounded by the soldiers of Beng Kher," said the partisan of Bharata Rahon who had before spoken. "Several escaped the audience chamber when your men entered, and already they have taken word to the warriors in the barracks. Presently they will come and you and your warriors will be destroyed."

"Perhaps," assented King; "but with us, then, shall die every man in this room, for I hold you as hostages to ensure our safety. If you are wise you will send a messenger at once to order your warriors to return to their barracks." And then to his own warriors he cried: "If a single warrior of Pnom Dhek enters this apartment without my authority, you will fall upon those here and slay them to a man, sparing only the women. And if my word is not sufficient I bring you the authority of your own King," and with that he displayed the King's ring, where all might see it.

Beaten at every turn, the followers of Bharata Rahon were forced to accept the inevitable, while those who had hated him were secretly delighted now that they were assured that both the Princess and the King had vouched for this strange warrior. Then in the great audience chamber of the Khmer King, Beng Kher, Fou-tan the Princess, dancing girl of the Leper King, was joined to the man she loved.

17

Conclusion

That night, for the first time in a thousand years perhaps, the soldiers of Lodidhapura and the soldiers of Pnom Dhek sat at the same board and laughed and joked and swore strange oaths and feasted and drank together; and the soldiers of Lodidhapura bragged of the prowess of their Prince, who single-handed and armed only with javelin had slain My Lord the Tiger; and the soldiers of Pnom Dhek boasted of the beauty of their Princess until presently those who were not sleeping beneath the table were weeping upon one another's brass cuirasses, so that when morning broke it was with aching heads that the soldiers of Lodidhapura climbed into the howdahs upon their great elephants and started back upon their homeward journey.

At the same time a strong force from Pnom Dhek, including many high officials of the court, together with the Princess Fou-tan and Gordon King, mounted upon swift elephants, set out through the jungle toward the dwelling of Che and Kangrey.

Upon the afternoon of the second day they reached their destination. Che and Kangrey and little Uda were overcome by the magnificence of the spectacle that burst suddenly upon their simple and astonished gaze; nor were they entirely free from apprehension until they had made sure that Gordon King was there to protect them.

"How is the patient, Kangrey?" asked King.

The woman shook her head. "He does not mend," she said.

Together Fou-tan and Gordon King, accompanied by the

199

high priest of Siva from Pnom Dhek and several of the highest officers of the court, entered the simple dwelling.

Beng Kher lay stretched upon his mean cot of straw and hides. His eyes lighted as they rested upon Fou-tan, who ran forward and kneeled beside him. The old warrior took her in his arms and pressed her to him, and though he was very weak he insisted that she tell him all that had transpired since King had left him to return to Pnom Dhek.

When she had finished, he sighed and stroked her hair; and when he motioned to Gordon King, and the man came and knelt at Fou-tan's side, Beng Kher took their hands in his.

"Siva has been kind to me in my last hour," he said. "He has saved Pnom Dhek and Fou-tan from the traitor, and he has given me a new son to rule when I am dead. All praise be to Siva."

The King, Beng Kher, closed his eyes. A tremor passed through his frame, which seemed suddenly to shrink and lie very still.

Gordon King lifted the weeping Fou-tan to her feet. The highest officer of the Khmer court came and knelt before them. He took the hand of Gordon King in his and pressed it to his lip. "I salute the son of Beng Kher," he said, "the new King of Pnom Dhek."

A NOTE TO ERB ENTHUSIASTS

For readers interested in learning more about the life and work of Edgar Rice Burroughs, Del Rey includes the following list of ERB fan clubs and their magazines. Write to the addresses below for information on memberships and subscriptions.

British Edgar Rice Burroughs Society
77 Pembroke Road
Seven Kings
Ilford, Essex
IG3 8PQ England

Burroughs Bibliophiles
Burroughs Memorial Collection
University of Louisville
Louisville, Kentucky 40292

Erbania
8001 Fernview Lane
Tampa, Florida 33615

ERB Collector
7315 Livingston Road
Oxon Hill, Maryland 20745

ERB-Fan
Eschenweg 5
8070 Ingolstadt
West Germany

ERB News Dateline
1990 Pine Grove Drive
Jenison, Michigan 49428

Tarzine
914 Country Club Drive
Midland, Texas 79701

About the Author

Edgar Rice Burroughs is one of the world's most popular authors. With no previous experience as an author, he wrote and sold his first novel—*A Princess of Mars*—in 1912. In the ensuing thirty-eight years until his death in 1950, Burroughs wrote ninety-one books and a host of short stories and articles. Although best known as the creator of the classic *Tarzan of the Apes* and *John Carter of Mars*, his restless imagination knew few bounds. Burroughs's prolific pen ranged from the American West to primitive Africa and on to romantic adventure on the moon, the planets, and even beyond the farthest star.

No one knows how many copies of ERB books have been published throughout the world. It is conservative to say, however, that with the translations into thirty-two known languages, including Braille, the number must run into the hundreds of millions. When one considers the additional worldwide following of the Tarzan newspaper feature, radio programs, comic magazines, motion pictures, and television, Burroughs must have been known and loved by literally a thousand million or more.